DATE

I'M EXPLODING NOW

I'M EXPLODING NOW

SID HITE

Hyperion
NEW YORK

Printed in the United States of America
First Edition
1 3 5 7 9 10 8 6 4 2
Library of Congress Cataloging-in-Publication Data on file.

ISBN-13: 978-0-7868-3757-1
ISBN-10: 0-7868-3757-8

This book is set in Adobe Caslon.
Designed by Ellice M. Lee
Reinforced binding

Visit www.hyperionteens.com

for Aidan Hite, a real teenager
and
Allie Hite, soon to be

PART ONE

The City

Max Whooten is my name. I'm sixteen and live on the Upper West Side of New York City. I was once real popular and my friends were always saying I was a funny guy, but no one has told me that lately because (A) my friends have either had mental breakdowns, (B) moved away, or (C) aren't my friends anymore, or (D) because I've been off my game and getting mad over nothing the past few months and don't have very many funny things to say.

It sucks, being off your game. People can see it a mile away and avoid you when they do, which puts you even further off your game. Then it's down, down, down you go into frustrationville.

* * *

I'm not stupid. At least that's my opinion. I know life is a chance to have fun, and only an idiot would spend all his time being mad at stuff. I know this in my head. Still, I can't seem to shake that frustrated feeling.

Something has to change. The way my life is going, I don't know how I'll make it through the summer. Hope it's just a phase.

two

Dad just told me if I didn't quit being so morose he was going to jump out the window. I said, "Go ahead. Make me happy." That ticked him off, and he asked what'd I know about happiness. I said, "Not much when you're around." It was a spiteful thing to say. I'm to blame for the shouting match we just had.

I don't hate Dad. Not on paper. He just has a talent for annoying me. He says I have a short fuse. I think it's a mutual problem.

I found *morose* in the dictionary. It means "having a sullen and gloomy disposition." Okay. Maybe I'm guilty of that. But hey, turn on the news. Morons are taking over the world. Of course I'm morose. Lucky I'm not depressed. Plenty of folks are.

I live with three neurotic people and an ancient cat that should have died years ago. The neurotics are my mom, dad, and fourteen-year-old sister, Cory. The cat's name is Mozart. I call him Crappy since all he does is eat, sleep, and crap everywhere but the litter box.

It's dangerous living with neurotic people, because if you aren't careful, they can be contagious. You might start out in the morning feeling normal and then by five o'clock be convinced you have a brain tumor. The only real protection against neurotic people is earplugs.

Mom says it breaks her heart when Dad and I fight. She's a pacifist who believes being nice to people solves everything. I feel sorry for Mom. Nice may have worked back in Iowa, where she's from, but it backfires here in New York. People in the city just smile and run Mom over, even the little preschoolers she teaches.

She thinks my diet is throwing me off. The other day she asked me to try eating an apple or a carrot, or anything besides the junk I live on. At first I laughed, but then she said, "Please, Max." So I ate an apple and half a cucumber, and a little later I drank a glass of water and tasted some of Cory's favorite peach yogurt.

It didn't make the slightest bit of difference. I still felt rotten.

A lot of so-called experts say teenagers suffer from too many hormones. They say the hormones explode in our blood and make us act weird. I'm tired of hearing it. Plenty of teenagers I know act weird just on principle.

I'm ticked today because school let out four days ago and it just hit me that I have nothing to do all summer. I should've seen it coming—I know, I have a calendar. But no. I put off thinking about summer until summer came.

One of the problems with being frustrated is you forget to think ahead.

It wouldn't have mattered anyway, even if I did think ahead. I don't have any money, and I'd still be living with three neurotic people and a pathetic cat.

I was furious when I came into my room and started

writing. I'm calmer now. Writing was Aunt Ginny's idea. She lives upstate near Woodstock and teaches yoga. Calm is her big thing. She said to get a notebook and write every time I have the I'm-exploding feeling I told her about. She said writing will help organize my thoughts.

I asked why should I organize a bunch of useless thoughts, and she said, "Because organizing your thoughts will help you understand your emotions, and understanding your emotions is the key to controlling them, and if you don't control yourself, someone else will."

I told her that that sounded good, except I didn't know how to write. She huffed at that and said, "If you can read, Max, you can write, and if you can't read by now, there's no help for you."

Then I asked, what should I write?

And she said, "Whatever you're thinking or have been doing. Anything. Just pretend you're speaking to the world."

Aunt Ginny's advice is usually worth taking, so I told her I'd give writing a try. I have to admit, it does make me calmer.

Speaking of calm, Dad is Aunt Ginny's brother, and he told me calm doesn't come natural to her. He said Aunt Ginny's natural condition is somewhere between hysterical and a conniption fit.

three

My friend Leila Kazilonif says people in New York live in boxes, work in boxes, sit in square parks, and think box-shaped thoughts. I've known Leila all my life. She lived in our building until last January when her dad took off. Then she and her mom moved downtown. Leila said switching schools midyear was worse than her dad splitting. He wasn't her dad anyway. She never met her real father.

The box I live in is on Eighty-fourth Street, five doors down from Broadway. Our mailbox in the lobby has pink and blue flowers on it. Cory painted the flowers and a little sign that says THE WHOOTENS. I absolutely refuse to pick up the mail.

* * *

Our apartment is on the ninth floor, so it makes sense that Dad got upset yesterday when I told him to jump, although only a moron wouldn't have known I was joking. I'm not calling Dad a moron. He just acts like one sometimes.

Dad worked for an elevator company for twelve years. It was a good job with all kinds of benefits, but he quit two weeks after 9/11 happened. He said it was time for him to be himself. Now he's an actor, which is almost the same as not having a job. Agreeable Mom supported his decision. She said Dad had been a struggling actor when they met, and if he wanted to be one again, she wouldn't be the one to stand in his way.

Dad got a few commercials in the beginning and worked on a soap opera for about three months, which was impressive since a lot of actors never get any work at all. Anyhow, things went pretty well for Dad for about a year. Then all of a sudden, no one would hire him. He's afraid he's too old for young-man parts and too young for old-man parts. Plus, he blames his agent.

Nowadays when Dad isn't complaining about everything that's wrong with show business, he worries about not having money. I know all about not having money. It's one of the few subjects where Dad and I can relate.

It sucks that I'm sitting in my room tonight writing about Dad. A guy with a girlfriend wouldn't be writing about his dad.

four

Things are going from bad to worse. Today a girl I sort of like(d) named Ana Middlen told me impecunious guys turned her off. I asked what impecunious meant, and she said it was being in the habit of never having any money. It was such a bizarre thing for her to say, I couldn't think of a comeback.

I never liked Ana that much to begin with. I just think she's sexy and wanted to make time with her.

That was earlier. This evening I made Cory cry without trying. She came into my room wearing a new skirt and blouse she'd just bought, and wondered what I thought about her outfit. I was honest. I told her it looked like expensive trash. Next thing I knew, she broke into tears, called me a heartless creep, and stormed out of my room. I tried later to apologize, but she covered her ears.

Cory will be fifteen at the end of July. She thinks having breasts is the key to the universe. She grew a pair last year, and now she's full of sophisticated opinions. Worse, she has a job in a flower shop and makes two hundred dollars a week.

Great. I squeak by on an allowance of sixty dollars a month while Cory drops hundreds on new outfits. What really worries me is that she'll probably have sex before I do. I'm not saying Cory is easy, but she's cute enough, and guys are already after her. Great. The way my luck is running, I'll never do the deed.

There's one thing I'd like to do almost as much as the deed, and that is figure out how Crappy poops under the couch in the living room. It's only three inches off the floor, yet he somehow manages to crap under there at least once a week. How he does it is a family mystery. No one has ever caught him in the act.

I've been thinking about this a lot. My guess is

that Crappy craps on the floor behind the couch, then goes away and lets it dry, then returns later and shoves the turd underneath with a paw. It's the only logical explanation.

five

I went downtown and hung with Leila today in Union Square. It was full of people doing nothing. Leila and I fit right in. We just sat on a bench and watched faces. Leila can be hilarious. She has such a wicked eye.

She cracked up when I told her what Ana Middlen said about impecunious guys. Leila is basically the opposite of materialistic. She's not a big fan of Ana either, but that's another story.

Leila and I had a long talk about our friend Trevor, who lost the plot last April and had a meltdown. It began with him saying things like "Got a hole in my soul" and "People are illusions." That wouldn't have been too bad, except his eyes bulged when he talked, and he couldn't stop scratching his face.

Trevor's parents already thought he was nuts because last year he got a tattoo on his chest that says GO GOD. It was a radical thing to do, and I sort of understand why his parents sent him to a hospital when he started scratching his face. Anyhow, a team of experts at the hospital shot Trevor so full of drugs he couldn't even find his face, much less scratch it. He was gone two weeks and basically hasn't been right since he came home.

Leila and I made plans to visit Trevor the day after tomorrow. She said, "We're probably his only friends, Max. If we don't visit him, no one will."

That's Leila. She's always been thoughtful of others. What's new about her is, she grew up to be a real babe. She's tall and skinny with a great figure, gorgeous black hair, and a really pretty face. I tease her that she looks like a Russian princess. Her mom is from the Ukraine.

I'm glad for Leila's sake that she's beautiful, but it's a drag for me because we've been friends since we were old enough to crawl, and it would probably seem warped if I tried to kiss her now. I think she agrees. I talked to her about it a couple of months ago, and she didn't argue that I was wrong.

Just my luck. I'm platonic friends with one of the hottest chicks in New York.

Leila is a poet. Her stuff is pretty good. She has ideas to go with her feelings and a real ear for words. My favorite poem she wrote is called "Just Around the Corner." It's about optimistic people always thinking their lives are going to get better any minute. She read me part of a new one she's been working on, "Ambition Condition." It's about all the automatons in the city that rush up and down the sidewalk talking on cell phones, except they don't actually have anything to say or anywhere to go.

When I was coming home on the subway this evening I saw a guy wearing a hooded sweatshirt, and it reminded me of this dream I've been having. It's not a sleep dream. It comes after I've gone to bed and am in the zone between awake and asleep. It might be called a fantasy. I've only had it three or four times.

It goes like this: There's a dance at our school and

everybody there is all dressed up. I come out of the bathroom and head back to where the band is playing. But it's not playing anymore. A guy is standing in the doorway with a machine gun. He's wearing a hood and black boots. Looks like a terrorist. I don't think. I charge and tackle the guy from behind, and while I've got him down, Arty Bernstein and Clay Quimby come and pin the guy's arms. I pick up the gun and aim it at the terrorist while a bunch of people call 911. The cops come fast. I give them the gun, and they take the guy away. Someone shouts, "Hooray for Max. He saved us!" Then everybody starts cheering and crowding around me, and I hang my head like it was nothing. It's a great way to fall asleep. All the girls love me and want to dance.

The weird part of the dream is Arty Bernstein grabbing the terrorist. Not only is Arty extremely shy, he's a squirt. I don't know why I keep putting him in the dream. Maybe I'm subconsciously trying to boost his confidence.

six

Dad was in the living room watching the news when I got up. He had on a suit. I asked if he'd gotten a job or something. He said the suit was for a part and he had an audition this afternoon. So I told him, "Break a leg," which is how you wish actors good luck. He said he appreciated my support. It was the best we've gotten along in ages.

I watched the news for a while after Dad left. I counted two wars, four murders, one sex scandal, two corporate corruptions, one natural disaster, and a brand-new disease. Same old stuff. The only thing missing was a baby kidnapping. The disease makes your bones shrink. I already forgot what it's called.

I'm cynical. I know that. What I don't know is, were things always so screwed up, or is it just in my lifetime? Sure looks to me like the world is going down the toilet.

I better find something to do before I go out of my head with boredom. Don't want to wind up like Trevor, although I think his problem is bigger than boredom. You don't go crazy like he did just because you have nothing to do.

Part of my problem is, I don't know what to do with my life. I mean, I know I want a girlfriend and some money, but that doesn't tell me what to do in my spare time.

You know how some little kids love dinosaurs and learn all their scientific names? Well, my sister Cory was that way with flowers. Before she could even walk, she got excited and screamed every time she saw a flower, which she did a lot because there's a flower shop on the corner of our block. Mom says she used to get embarrassed pushing Cory past the florist in her baby carriage because Cory would make such a fuss, people on the street would give Mom suspicious looks, like maybe she was mistreating her child. Anyhow, later, after Cory got older, she hung around the shop so much the florist figured he might as well give her a job. His name is Kenneth. He's a nut job, but he's so happy about it everybody likes him.

The point I was trying to make is, Cory has always known what she wanted to do with her life, and that's pretty much the opposite of me. Of course, I've always known I wanted to have a blast, but that's something you do *in* life, not *with*. Besides, you can't have a blast when you're off your game. You just go bust when you try.

Questions to think about:

How do you know what to do when you don't know what you want to do?

How do you get back on your game when you're off?

Why and when did everything that used to seem so simple become so complicated?

The only thing I want to do right now is nothing. I would go up on the roof and do nothing, except our super won't allow it. He's a tyrant named Fendyke, and he's busted me twice for going up. Last time he caught me he

said he'd stuff me down the trash chute if I went up again.
I wouldn't put it past him. Fendyke is sick.

News flash: Max Whooten, a confused genius from the
Upper West Side of New York City, was found today, com-
pacted into a cube, on a trash barge headed for Rhode
Island.

seven

Leila called this morning and changed our day for visiting Trevor. We're going tomorrow. Whatever. It's just another day with nothing to do.

Mom only works part-time in summer, which means if Dad doesn't have an audition or a job, and if I don't go out, there are three of us hanging around the Whooten Box. It's an unhealthy situation, so I grabbed my notebook, stuck five dollars in my pocket, and went out.

I remember when I was little I thought five dollars was a lot of money. Right. About the only thing you can do on the Upper West Side with five dollars is buy a box of tissues, stand on the street, and blow your nose.

I cut over to Riverside Park and drifted uptown until I found an empty bench across from a nursery playground, which is where I'm sitting right now. It's a pretty interesting spot. In the last fifteen minutes I've seen five kids fall on their butts, two kids bang their heads together, and one little girl slip off the swing. Made me laugh out loud. I'd forgotten how clumsy little kids are.

Wake up. Cute chick coming this way.

Never mind. She's with that guy.

Tonight basically sucks. We ordered Chinese, then Mom and Dad went to a movie, Cory went shopping with her friend Athena DePree, and I stayed home watching television. Just me and Crappy.

Today when I was coming home, I stopped for a slice and saw a guy from school named Grant Whalen. I hardly know Grant, but he said, "Hey," so I said, "Hi," which was a mistake because he thought it meant he was invited to sit at my table and watch me eat. The guy was crunked on something. He didn't say a word, so after like two minutes I asked if he had plans for the summer. He grinned and said, "Plan to stay wasted."

Stoners like Grant are never as funny as they think they are. Anyhow, after I didn't say anything, he asked if I had plans for the summer. I said I was building a nuclear reactor on my roof. He just nodded and said, "Cool."

Later, I was coming down Broadway when a bum on the sidewalk said to give him a dollar. I told him to get lost, but of course he didn't. Instead he started following me like he was going to do something. I walked real slow until he caught up with me, then I spun around and shouted as loud as I could, "GOT A PROBLEM?" That must have surprised him, because he backed away fast and said, "Sorry, man. Thought I knew you."

You gotta watch it in New York. The place is crawling with creeps.

eight

I don't know what to say about Trevor. When Leila and I got to his place today and he opened the door, we said hello like normal people, and he said, "*Om mani padme hum.*" Leila and I thought he was joking and laughed. He looked hurt. Then he said, "I suppose you came to see if I'm still crazy."

Leila said, "No, Trevor, we came because we're your friends."

Trevor thought about that for a second, then smiled and told us to come on in. I could see from the way he smiled that he wasn't stable. We sat in the living room, and Trevor's mom stood in the kitchen trying to listen to everything we said. There wasn't much to hear at first. I asked how he was doing, and he said, "Depends on how much medicine I take."

There was a weird pause after that. I wanted to shout: *Does your mom still eavesdrop on everybody?* Instead I asked Trevor if his medicine was good. He said it was strong, and sounded so sad when he spoke I almost wanted to hug him or something. Poor guy looked pretty lost.

Then Leila said, "So, *om mani padme hum.* Is that Tibetan?" and Trevor perked up. He said, "It's from somewhere over there. By the way, did I tell you guys I'm a Buddhist now?" Leila and I shook our heads. We were both surprised and just sat listening when Trevor started babbling about how Buddhists are lamps unto themselves and don't have desires, and how some guy named Gautama lived on one grain of rice a day, plus a lot more that I can't remember. Trevor had obviously been reading up on the subject.

After he stopped talking, I said, "Are you sure about the one grain of rice? That's not much food."

Trevor said he was sure, then explained how enlightened people draw energy out of the air and don't require a lot of calories. It sounded kooky to me, but he believed what he was saying. I was thinking tonight about his GO GOD tattoo and thought Buddhism might be good for him. I mean, he couldn't be worse off than he was before. Maybe Buddha will get him off that medicine.

It was an intense visit, and Leila and I were relieved when we left. Neither of us said anything on the ride down in the elevator. Then, just as we were getting off in the lobby, Leila said, "Wouldn't shock me if Trevor is wearing a lampshade the next time we visit." That broke me up, and I couldn't stop laughing until we were two blocks away.

It's not funny, though. Trevor's my friend, and I should probably do something to help him. But what? He's not really in a condition for listening to reason. I'd knock him in the head with a brick if I thought it would help, but I doubt it would.

Just remembered something else Leila said today. We'd walked to the subway, and she was about to go down when I asked if she knew the meaning of life. She thought a second and put a hand on my arm and said, "I'll have to get back to you on that, Max."

I said, "Okay, but if you wanted to go looking for the meaning of life, where would you start?"

She said, "Philosophy, probably."

And I asked, "Not religion?"

Then she said, "Maybe religion. I don't know. I'm just a poet. But you're kind of philosophical, Max. My gut says you might find what you're looking for there."

Interesting, Leila saying I was philosophical. Never thought of myself that way before.

nine

I cussed out a shoe today because I couldn't get the lace through the hole where it was supposed to go. I'm not retarded. The plastic end was gone from the lace and it just wouldn't fit. Still, it was no excuse for swearing at a shoe. You can get sent to a nuthouse for stuff like that.

Come to think of it, I already live in a nuthouse.

Anyhow, after I finally got the stupid shoelace through the stupid hole in the stupid shoe, I left the Whooten Box and tried to see how far I could walk without caring where I was. Made it to Thirty-third Street before I turned around. Fifty-one blocks. Never said a word to anyone. Just walked and wondered about the meaning of life.

At one point I was looking at all the people on the sidewalk when I had the idea they were all thinking the same thing. *Who am I and what am I doing here?* It was mass weird. It made me want to shout, *All you morons, get back in your boxes!*

I didn't shout, of course. I may be off my game, but I'm still civilized. Besides, a lot of the people looked pretty down already, and I didn't want to make them feel worse.

Now that I've gotten into it, I'm enjoying keeping this notebook. I'd probably enjoy it more if something cool happened in my life, like finding a girl I liked who actually liked me. Then I could write about her, which would be a lot better than writing about down people on the sidewalk. It would be better for me, too. I mean, better besides the writing.

Who knows? If she was really cute and interesting, I might forget all about my notebook.

It would be okay too if she was extremely rich and super sexy. I wouldn't mind that at all.

ten

My computer crashed downloading music, so now I use Cory's to check my e-mail. Except I have to ask first, which is fair, but she's not here now and that sucks. What also sucks is, usually the only thing in my in-box is junk.

If I had money, I'd buy a new computer. Or maybe not. Maybe I'd buy a monkey. I always wanted a monkey. If I got one, I'd name him Pete and teach him funny tricks, and work the street for money.

Pete. The funny money monkey.

Watch it, Max. You're slipping.

* * *

I tried talking to Dad after dinner about the idea of money, but he thought I was bringing up the subject for selfish reasons, and said the best way to get money was to find a job. It was so typical of the way he thinks.

My problem with a job is, I like sleeping late when I'm not in school, and the only places that would hire me for late are fast-food joints, but they're out since I refuse to wear a hairnet.

I'm bored with my video games. Think I'll hock them.

eleven

Not a bad a day in the Whooten Box. First, Morey Slockin called to tell Dad the director of a movie he auditioned for last month wanted to see him again. It's called a callback. Actors love them. Morey is Dad's agent. He almost never has good news.

Dad knows better than to get excited. He said even if he lands the part, it's a low-budget film that will hardly pay his minimum day rate. Still, he was happy. It's been a while since I've seen him even close to happy.

Right after Dad hung up with Morey, Leila called to say she and her mom are going to spend a couple of weeks on a friend's farm in Pennsylvania. I said,

"What? You're leaving me here all alone?" She said, "Max. This is New York. Look out the window. You won't be alone."

Leila was psyched about going away. Said it had been ages since she'd seen a cow. She's leaving the day after tomorrow.

I was in the dumps after talking to Leila, but then Cory came home from work for lunch and told me Athena DePree was having a Fourth of July party. Even better, I'm invited.

Athena is Cory's best friend. She just turned fifteen but looks seventeen, and is definitely the cutest chick in Cory's crowd. Plus, Athena lives in a penthouse with a pool. It's a great place for a party.

I know Athena pretty well because she stayed with us for two weeks last summer when her parents went to France. We talked a lot when she was here and Cory was working, and I must say, for a rich babe, Athena is a good conversationalist. She knows how to listen without drifting off, and always says smart things when it's her turn to talk.

I know I shouldn't think this, but I wonder if Athena has a boyfriend.

FORGET IT, MAX. Cory and Athena tell each other everything, and Cory would kill you. You don't want that. Your life already sucks enough without being dead.

twelve

Sold nine video games for sixty-two dollars. It's a fraction of what they were worth, but that's business. You sell something you don't want to someone who wants it and take what you can get.

The worst part of the deal was the jerk at Game World. He couldn't just buy my games. First he had to ask where I stole them from and treat me like a dirtbag for coming into the store. I didn't say anything until I had the money in my hand. Then I told him it was morons like him who give human beings a bad name, and stomped out.

I was feeling rich when I got home, but I didn't know what to do. Then I remembered I wanted to find the meaning of life, so I went to the bookstore on Broadway and farted around in the philosophy section for a while. I didn't really expect to find the meaning of life for sale. I was just looking for clues.

The first book I picked up was on Socrates. He was a famous philosopher in Greece who was ugly and had a wife named Xanthippe who talked more than he did, which was something, because Socrates talked a lot. Anyhow, one thing he said when Xanthippe let him get a word in was, "Of the Gods we know nothing." Socrates was a pretty serious guy. He killed himself in a bathtub rather than agree he was wrong when he wasn't wrong.

After Socrates, I looked at some books on Plato and Aristotle. I guess they were wise like Socrates, but I couldn't really tell that from what I read. In fact, I almost fell asleep on my feet reading about a republic that Plato invented.

Basically, in my opinion, all the famous philosophers beat around the bush too much. They begin by stating what the question is, then make a list of rules for answering the question, then argue both sides of every detail to death. I kept thinking, *Come on, guys. Cut to the chase. Talk about the meaning of life.* But no. They went on and on about virtue and dignity and moral stuff like that, which was important to them, I guess, but not what I wanted to read.

It wasn't too long before I got tired of philosophy and drifted over to the religion section, which is between occult and self-help. I picked up a couple of books there and peeked inside, but only pretended to read a little because I just wasn't in a religious mood.

I'd decided to split and was heading toward the escalator when I saw a guy from school named Toshen Chenault. He said, "Hey, Max" when he saw me, which was a surprise because Toshen is a grade above me and the prince of the in-crowd, and I didn't think he even knew my name. But obviously he did, so I said, "Hey" to Toshen, and we wound up talking for maybe half an hour.

I usually don't notice if guys are handsome or not, but you can't help it when you're talking to Toshen because he looks just like an Abercrombie & Fitch model, only thinner. Of course he drives girls crazy and gets to pick whichever one he wants to go out with.

Most of the popular, good-looking people I know are snobs, but not Toshen. He treated me just like an equal, and soon I was feeling so relaxed talking to him, I asked did he have any tips for getting girls. He laughed when I asked that because he thought I was making a joke, but after he saw I was serious, he said there was no secret for getting girls. I told him there must be something to it. Then he thought for a few seconds and said, "Well, Max. Girls are pretty much like everybody else. They want your undivided attention. Just look them in their eyes when they talk, then say something that shows you were listening."

I thanked Toshen for the advice, but I must not have sounded very convinced, because he laughed again and slapped me on the back and said, "When I really, really want to seal the deal with a girl, I buy her chocolate. Works like a charm."

It's funny how things work, but hanging with Toshen in the bookstore today reminded me of what it was like to feel cool, and I felt that way for almost the whole rest of the day.

Feeling cool makes a lot of problems disappear. It's fun and beats the hell out of feeling off your game.

Just got back from Cory's room. I apologized for dissing her outfit the other day and said it was cute. Cory is smart, though, and she said, "Oh yeah. What color was my skirt?" I had to confess I forgot the exact color. She laughed at that and said I should prepare my white lies better. I told her, "Uh-huh," then said real casually, like I was talking about something that didn't matter, "So, Athena's party should be fun. How's she doing these days? She got a boyfriend?"

Cory rolled her eyes at the ceiling and said, "I haven't talked to Athena today, so things may have changed, but the last time I checked she had five boyfriends."

Good. Now I know Athena plays the field. Not that it matters. I'm not the least bit interested.

Whew. My hand hurts. Tonight was the most I've ever written.

thirteen

Having a bad morning. Woke up thinking about the moron from Game World and almost decided to go down there and kick his ass, but I didn't, because he was pretty big. Besides . . . well, it just wasn't the thing to do. Anyhow, after I got that waste of human parts off my mind, I called Trevor to tell him what Socrates said. His mom answered the phone and put me on hold forever, then clicked back in and said Trevor didn't want to talk. I have a feeling she never even told him I called.

Now what, you unemployed genius?

Get out of here.

* * *

I walked over to Central Park this afternoon and threw a Frisbee with two guys I met near Belvedere Castle. I was making some great catches and we were having mass fun before one of them said they had to go and they went. I never even knew their names. It reminded me I don't have many guy friends to hang with.

After Trevor, one of my friends I miss the most is Twig Kern, who moved to Colorado in March with his dysfunctional family. Twig is one of those guys who is always up for anything, even bad ideas, like trying to skateboard down the steps into the subway, which was how he broke an arm last summer. Funny guy, Twig. I wish there were more people like him.

I was going to take a bus home from the park, but after waiting like twenty minutes for a crosstown, I started walking, and of course that's when the bus came. I turned around and started running, but the driver took off before I got there, which really ticked me off, so I jumped in the street, screamed at him as loud as I could, and flipped the bird. The guy just grinned as he went past me. It's New York. Someone probably flips him the bird every day.

So I was standing there screaming at the bus when a taxi zipped by with a white-haired woman in the back. Her face wasn't ten inches away, and I could see her studying me like I was some kind of wild tourist attraction. I didn't know whether to laugh or cry, but it made me feel special.

Walking home didn't bother me too much. I do some of my best thinking while I walk. Today I was thinking that everyone wants to be happy, yet only a few people are, and even those people aren't happy all the time. Then I thought, a guy could earn a fortune if he invented something that automatically made people happy. I was pretty excited about the idea at first. Inventing a happiness-maker seemed the perfect thing to do with my life, except for one problem. I couldn't think of anything new to invent. I mean, they already make pills to keep you from being sad, and electric shock therapy has been around for ages, and . . . well, I just couldn't come up with any fresh ideas.

Athena's party is in five days. It's the first fun thing on my calendar since I don't know when. Hope I get lucky at the

Crappy came and sat in my lap a few minutes ago. He does it now and then. It's his way of reminding me he was once a normal kitten. First he sits on my crotch, leans his head against my stomach, and tries to purr. Except he can't purr anymore. Instead he makes a wheezing noise that sounds like he's choking on a hair ball. So he wheezes until he can't take it any longer, then he stands up, digs his claws in my legs, and jumps. He didn't do it tonight, but sometimes, just before he jumps, Crappy will lift his tail and fart at me.

Listen, world: If there is anybody out there who doesn't have a cat and is thinking about getting a kitten for a pet, DON'T. It will just be rude to you when it grows up.

fourteen

Aunt Ginny was in the city to see a doctor today and paid the Whooten Box a visit when she was done. Said she was fine, it was a just a routine checkup. She looked okay to me.

Everyone was home when she came, and we didn't get a chance to talk, so I rode the subway with her to Grand Central, where she catches an upstate train. Dad acted shocked when I offered to go. Said he didn't know I was a gentleman. I told him there was more he didn't know where that came from. It got a chuckle out of Mom.

Hanging with Aunt Ginny is the same as hanging with

someone my age, except she can concentrate longer and isn't conceited. She told me she likes being called Aunt Ginny, instead of just Ginny. Said it added formality to her unconventional life. I think she regrets not getting married and having kids.

We talked about my writing and how it was maybe organizing something in my head, then she hooked arms with me and asked who my girlfriend was. I usually try to be honest, so I said I didn't have a girlfriend. Aunt Ginny shook her head and said, "What's wrong with girls these days? Are they blind?"

I said, "They can see all right. They just don't like me."

It was a couple of seconds before Aunt Ginny could think of a reply. When she did, she said, "They obviously don't know you, Max. They'd be lining up around the block if they did."

Her saying that didn't make me feel any better. In fact, a lot of times when people say something to try to cheer you up it rubs in the reason you're not cheerful, and makes things worse. I'm not suggesting people be mean to each other. That would never work. They just have to be careful with compliments they give out and make sure they don't sound like pity.

Anyhow, I hung with Aunt Ginny until they called her train. She gave me a Woodstock hug before leaving. I think she invented the hug. It's a full wraparound squeeze.

I went grocery shopping for Mom tonight, which I don't mind doing since I get to pick my own snacks. While I was there I saw Arty Bernstein shopping with his mom. I'd never seen her before. She had on sunglasses and looked like some kind of retired movie star. She pushed the cart and made Arty get items she pointed to off the shelves. Then, if she didn't like the item close up, Arty had to put it back and get something else. I'm glad for Arty's sake he didn't see me watching. His mom was treating him like a slave. Later I bumped into them at the checkout. Made a point of being real friendly to Arty and even told his mom, "You know, Mrs. Bernstein, Arty is the best musician in our school."

She looked at me like I worked in the store or

something and said, "He ought to be, after ten years of private lessons."

Arty cringed when she said that. Made me wish I hadn't brought the subject up.

fifteen

Shouldn't have bought all that junk food at the store last night. I felt rotten all day and feel rotten tonight.

Dad thinks he landed the part in the movie, although he won't know for sure until next week. Maybe that'll get him off my case.

My case. What case? I hardly have a life.

Something serious might be wrong with me. I feel so rotten right now, I can't even think about sex.

Hope I don't die.

* * *

Don't die yet, Max. Wait until you at least have a girlfriend to cry at your funeral.

sixteen

Threw up first thing this morning. Feel much better now.

Haven't spent the money I got for my games yet. Think I need a new shirt for Athena's party. I'm scary when I shop for clothes. Last time I went, I bought two really cool shirts in the store, but when I got home, I realized they were geeky. I found them in my closet the other night. I also found a petrified cat turd that must be six months old. It's still in the closet with the stupid shirts.

I went to American Eagle Outfitters today and looked at a bunch of ridiculously priced shirts. After about an hour and the salesguy asking me ten times if he could help me, I decided to wear my old blue V-neck to Athena's party and keep my money. I walked from American Eagle to Times Square and had a slice, then stood out on the street watching people. New Yorkers never go to Times Square unless they work there. Almost everyone you see is a tourist. They're so easy to spot, they might as well wear signs that say *I'm from out of town and this is my idea of fashion.*

I have to say, some of those out-of-towners looked pretty hot. There was one group of girls I couldn't keep my eyes off of. Two of them had on halter tops you could practically see through. I know because I tried. Funny thing was, the girls knew what I was doing, and kept turning in my direction to make sure I got a good look. I almost walked over and thanked them for the show just before I left.

Later, I was cutting across Forty-eighth Street near Sixth Avenue when I saw four guys coming out of Manny's Music Store. They all had long hair and were wearing lots of jewelry, and looked like they hardly ever saw the sun. I didn't recognize them or anything, but I got the feeling they were a famous band. It made sense because there are pictures of a lot of famous musicians who shop at Manny's on the walls. Jimi Hendrix used to go there a lot when he was alive. I'm big on Hendrix. He was the best.

Anyhow, I went in Manny's to look around, and while I was in there I almost put a deposit on a set of used congas. I don't have any natural rhythm for playing the congas. I just wanted them for torturing Cory.

seventeen

I haven't been getting any e-mails, so I figured I'd write some and see if anyone answered. I had to call Cory at the shop and get permission to use her computer. She said okay, just not to go through her stuff. I don't know why she'd think I'd do that.

I don't know if there's a computer where Leila is staying in Pennsylvania, but I wrote her and said I hoped she'd seen a cow.

Then I wrote to Twig in Colorado and said I hadn't written him so far this summer because I was busy having mass fun. I don't like lying to friends, but I didn't want to bore him with the lousy truth. I told him about Athena's party tomorrow night, and said it was too bad he'd moved to the middle of nowhere. Twig always busts people's chops. I wanted to get in the first jab.

I was going to write Trevor, but that seemed lame, so I called him. Fortunately, his gargoyle mom didn't answer. He said he'd cut down on his medicine and maybe felt a bit better, then told me he'd signed up for a seminar on Buddhism at the New School.

I had to laugh. The old Trevor wouldn't have signed up for a seminar unless his life depended on it. Maybe it does.

Trevor wasn't interested when I told him I'd been reading some philosophy and that Socrates said, "Of the gods we know nothing." He said Socrates didn't hold a wet match to Buddha. I didn't argue with Trevor because of his condition, but I thought it was a rude thing to say about Socrates.

A strange thing happened in the Whooten Box tonight. Instead of me and Dad fighting, Cory and Mom had a shouting match in the kitchen. I sat in my room with the door open and listened. I think Dad was listening from the living room because I heard him turn the volume down on the TV. The fight was about an article that Mom made Cory read. It was on teens hooking up for sex at parties.

Cory thought the article was a disgusting farce that had nothing to do with the truth, plus she didn't appreciate Mom's method of communicating. She said, "If you have something to say to me, Mom, say it. Don't make me read something in a magazine."

Mom said she was just passing along what seemed like interesting reading material.

Then Cory screamed, "If that's true, why'd you insist I read it and tell you what I thought?"

Mom told Cory to mind her tone of voice.

Cory said, "Go ahead, Mom. Tell me what's on your mind."

Mom said, "Okay. Have you hooked up at any parties?" It was interesting, Mom asking that the night before Athena's party.

Anyhow, Cory forgot her tone of voice again and shouted, "THAT IS NONE OF YOUR BUSINESS!"

They went back and forth about whose business was whose for like ten minutes, then Cory got tired of arguing

and explained that her crowd was into romantic relation-
ships, and only immature kids with problems hooked up
with people they hardly knew. That seemed to satisfy
Mom, and after that she and Cory talked so quietly, Dad
and I couldn't hear them.

I have to give Cory credit. She sure knows how to
manage Mom.

If Dad gives me any articles about sex with girls, they
better have color pictures. I'm not reading them if they
don't.

eighteen

Just tore out the last four pages in my notebook. They were all about what a pathetic loser I am for screwing up at Athena's party.

I hate feeling like a loser.

At least I figured out that the meaning of life is there is no meaning, except you have to suffer. Plus, you meet a lot of morons along the way.

The truth is a pain in the ass sometimes.

nineteen

Athena's party was four nights ago. I've been trying to laugh it off, but I can't.

I have this thing where I get a huge amount of energy before parties. I'm not sure where it comes from, but it builds up in me and doesn't go away until after I get to where the party is and start talking to people. Then I usually feel normal again . . . whatever normal is.

I waited forty-five minutes after Cory left before heading to Athena's. I was pretty wound up when I got to the place, but then Mrs. DePree opened the door and remembered my name and acted so friendly, I started feeling all right. She called Athena, who came right away and gave me an air kiss. Then we walked out to the pool deck together.

Making my appearance with Athena felt great. She had on a very short skirt and a sexy top, and had a perfect tan to go with her perfect hair. I swear she gets cuter every time I see her.

When we stepped out onto the pool deck, I saw Cory talking to a guy named Ryan, who she likes. I waved and she waved back, and everything was cool. But then Athena's preppy cousin from Connecticut walked over, and she introduced us. His name is Otto and he was wearing a pin-striped shirt. I'd never met him before and had nothing against him, so I stuck out my hand and said hi, but the arrogant jerk didn't even bother to lift his arm. He just looked me over and said, "What do you do, Max?"

I wasn't ready for that kind of question, so I said, "I don't do much. You could say I'm retired."

He sort of smirked and said, "Retired from nothing, eh? That takes talent."

That ticked me off and I said, "What about you, Otto? Were you born stupid, or was there an accident?"

He pretended to be amused and said, "Actually, I'm rather intelligent."

I couldn't let that slide and told him, "That's strange, because you look like a dumb-ass."

Then it got confusing because he and Athena talked at the same time. He was saying it was better to look dumb than be dumb, and she was saying maybe Otto and I should step back and start over. It didn't matter what they were saying because it was too late for me to stop myself, and I exploded. I grabbed one of Otto's arms, spun him around real fast, and slung him into the pool. I'm not an athlete or anything, but I used to do forty push-ups a day, and I'm pretty strong when I want to be.

Everyone went dead silent when Otto hit the water, and I saw Cory looking horrified across the pool at me.

Then Otto popped up and screamed, "YOU MANIAC! Hey, everybody. Max is insane."

Athena and I looked at each other, but she didn't say a word, then we both watched Otto climb out of the pool. What I didn't see was that he had a buddy who snuck around behind me and threw a sucker punch at my head.

I ducked just in time for the punch to miss me, then jumped sideways and yanked back my elbow. I got lucky and knocked the wind right out of the guy. He went "Ahhhh," and sat on the floor.

Next thing I knew, everyone was staring at me, and Otto was screaming, "Someone call the cops. There's a maniac on the loose."

It was obviously time for me to go, so I told Athena I hoped I hadn't ruined her party and headed for the door.

The only good thing that happened was when I walked past Mrs. DePree, she winked and said, "Well done, Max. I've been wanting to throw that brat in the pool since he learned to talk."

Anyway . . . that was my fifteen minutes at probably the best party I'll be invited to this year. I didn't eat anything, didn't dance with anybody, didn't see the fireworks, and didn't have any fun. On top of that, Cory chewed me out the next day and said she didn't want to have anything to do with me socially for the rest of her life. When I tried to mention that at least I was invited to the party and didn't crash it, she screamed, "Because of me, you mal-adjusted freak."

I know Cory had a good excuse for being mad, but that hurt.

twenty

All I did today was watch TV with the sound off and eat a big bag of potato chips. All I've done tonight is lie on the floor thinking what a piece of crap my life is.

They say you get what you deserve. I should go up on the roof and let Fendyke stuff me down the trash chute.

Maybe Dad was right. Maybe my fuse is too short.

Philosophical question: Do fuses grow out of people's heads, or their stomachs, or their butts?

twenty-one

I took a long time getting out of bed today. I just lay there thinking about Athena's party and that I don't have a job, or any money, or a girlfriend, and that my computer had crashed. While I was thinking that, Crappy pushed open my door, came over to my bed, and farted as if it was the most natural thing to do. Then he turned around and strolled proudly out of the room.

It's strange, but Crappy farting at me while I was lying in bed thinking downer thoughts made me realize my life couldn't get any worse than it had gotten, and if it couldn't get worse, it had to get better, and that cheered me up.

Moods are amazing. I popped out of bed after Crappy left and did fifteen push-ups.

Since Cory and I aren't talking, I can't ask permission to use her computer, so I went to an Internet cafe this afternoon to check for e-mails. I had one from Twig, who I am glad to say is the same goofball he always was. He told me everybody in Colorado was awed because he was from New York City, and his only problem these days was remembering the names of his new girlfriends. Then he asked if I had a girlfriend yet, and how was Athena's party. I said everybody skinny-dipped in the pool, but I got bored and left. Then I told him I didn't want to talk about my girlfriend because she caught pneumonia doing an underwear modeling job last week and died.

Dad was lying on the living-room floor with his arms flopped to the sides when I got home this afternoon. I asked him what he was doing, and he said, "Celebrating." I said, "Celebrating what, the ceiling?" He said, "No, prosperity." Then he explained how on top of learning yesterday that he'd landed the part in that movie he auditioned for, he found out today that he'd gotten cast in an extremely well-paying, national headache commercial. Dad's good at headaches. They're his speciality. I told him, "Right on."

Mom came into my room tonight and asked could we talk. I knew before she started that she was worried about me. I don't mind Mom or Dad getting annoyed with me, but it makes me cringe when they worry because they think I have a problem. Doesn't matter if I have one or not. I just don't like them thinking I do.

Anyhow, first thing Mom said was, "I heard about your fight at Athena's party."

I told her, "I threw a moron in the pool and made one of his friends sit down; it wasn't a fight."

Mom bobbed her head. Then she said that me hanging around the apartment all summer wasn't doing anyone any good, and she'd pay for the registration if I wanted to sign up for a class somewhere. When I asked what kind of class did she have in mind, she said, "It's up to you, Max. Is there something you're interested in?"

I said, "Yeah, girls." Mom sort of cracked a smile at that. Then I told her I'd think about her idea and let her know.

Mom's okay.

twenty-two

Today is Sunday. It's been a week and a day since Leila left. I miss her. She's one of the only people I know who isn't out just to serve herself. She told me once that when she gets older she wants to go to a poor country and help handicapped kids lead normal lives.

An idea like that would never cross my mind. Makes me think girls might be better people than guys. The only reason a guy would go to a poor country was if the girls there were pretty, and known to be wild.

I know it's not that simple. I mean, some guys are sensitive and do generous stuff, and some girls are selfish and only want to go shopping. My point is, Leila thinks about more than just what can make her happy, and that's cool.

Mom asked me tonight if I'd given any more thought to taking a class. I said I'd make a decision tomorrow. Don't know why I told her that. I haven't thought about it.

I doubt any teenager in the world except someone from New York City takes classes in summer, unless they flunked a grade and didn't want to repeat the next year. In the city, though, everybody is always trying to improve themselves, plus you can go crazy when there's nothing to do, so people sign up for classes to kill time. That's my theory.

Another thing about teenagers in the city, they have a lot of personal problems. Look at Trevor—and I could name a bunch more who are screwed up too. If you're from New York and you don't have a nervous disorder by the time you're fifteen, everybody wants to know what's wrong with you.

Ha.

Live in a box, think square thoughts, and sign up for classes with a bunch of blockheaded people who have nothing else to do.

twenty-three

I already knew I had rotten luck, but after what happened today, I think I'm cursed.

I woke up this morning with a voice in my head that said, "The tae kwon do school on Seventy-sixth Street." Sounded like a good idea to me, learning how to kick people in the head.

So after lunch I walked down to Seventy-sixth and went in the building where they teach tae kwon do, and saw a really cute blonde standing by the elevator. She smiled and the door opened, then we got on together and she hit the floor button. She was wearing leotards and a T-shirt that said MOTION, and was so sexy I didn't think about where I was going. All I thought was, *She can kick me in the head if she wants.*

After a few seconds she said, "Hi. I'm Iris. Are you here for a class?" I told her my name was Max and said I planned to sign up for one. Then the elevator stopped and she told me, "I work here, Max. I can show you what's available and get you registered."

I followed her like a sheep down the hallway. I should've known something was wrong when she said over her shoulder, "We don't get many guys your age." But I wasn't thinking.

I didn't have to think when we went in her office and I saw all the posters and stuff. Talk about feeling stupid. I'd gotten off on the fourth floor instead of the third, where the tae kwon do school is, and was in the office of a dance school.

I wasn't done being stupid, either, because when Iris gave me a brochure with all the classes I could take, I was too embarrassed to tell her I'd made a mistake, and pretended to study the brochure like I was interested. Finally, after I didn't say anything for about a minute, she asked, "Anything grab you?"

I don't know where my brain was, but my mouth said, "Tap dancing looks cool."

Damn those cute girls. They make me helpless. I filled out a form and told Iris that Wednesdays and Fridays looked good for me, and I'd stop by tomorrow with a deposit for the shoes I'm supposed to buy.

I was in such a rush getting out of the building, I didn't even peek in at the tae kwon do school.

Tired of everything going wrong. I can't even sign up for a class without screwing up.

Hope I have my hero dream tonight.

twenty-four

Called Trevor today, but his mom said he was out. Probably eating lotus petals with some Buddha freaks he met at that seminar.

I told Mom this afternoon I wouldn't be taking any classes because I'd be going to the library twice a week to study philosophy.

She said, "Aren't you full of surprises?"

I called the dance school this afternoon and told the woman who answered the phone I was going on vacation with my dad and wouldn't be coming to the tap class I signed up for. She said, "Oh. Where're you going?" I said, "Brazil."

It's a shame Iris was so cute. Now if I see her on the street, I'll have to hide.

Maybe I should walk to Colorado and drop in on Twig.

twenty-five

One good thing about New York is the library on Fortieth and Fifth Avenue. It's huge, you don't need a card to go in and look around, plus there's a park out back where cute girls sometimes hang.

I went today and asked the guy in the reference room if he could recommend a book on philosophy. He wasn't very old, maybe college age. He asked what branch of philosophy was I interested in. I wasn't up on my branches and said, "You know, one of the meaning-of-life branches." The guy gave me a superior look and said I had to be more specific, so I asked him to name some branches. Then he spit out a long list of words that all ended in "ism." There was nihilism, behaviorism, existentialism, idealism, pragmatism, structuralism, and I forget what else. I think the guy had just been dying for someone to come in and ask about philosophical branches.

Anyhow, I was standing there trying to decide what to say, when it hit me that I was a sixteen-year-old guy with all my parts in working order, and the meaning of my life ought to be to just cool out and see what happens. So I said adios to the librarian and went out to sit in Bryant Park.

Bryant Park is excellent people-watching, especially on really hot days like today when girls don't wear much and are so busy sweating they forget to be self-conscious. I was concentrating on cooling out, though, and didn't let myself get too distracted by any sweaty girls.

One thing I learned today was, when you're trying to cool out, don't sit on an iron bench in the sun. I don't know how long it took me to notice it, but at one point I reached up to touch the top of my head and it felt like my hair was on fire.

I moved to a shady spot then, but my hair was still hot, and that got me thinking about fuses again. Then it occurred to me that if mine were on my head, it had probably ignited, and I might explode any second. So I started counting down. *Ten, nine, eight,* and so on, until *zero,* at which point nothing happened. I wasn't disappointed, though. It was fun just thinking about something besides all that needs fixing in my pathetic life.

One thing that definitely needs fixing is Cory. I saw her in the hallway a little while ago and she didn't even bother to glare at me. It can't go on, both of us living in the same box and not talking. The math doesn't work.

I'd apologize for embarrassing her at Athena's party if she'd let me, but she won't.

twenty-six

Some people wake up to the sound of birds tweeting. I woke up this morning to Dad shouting from outside my door, "Max, when are you going to learn to pull the curtain when you shower?"

I told him, "Wrong again, Dad. I haven't showered for two days. Quit accusing me of stuff I didn't do."

He said, "Oh. Well, pull the curtain next time you shower."

I hate being accused of stuff I didn't do. It's exactly that kind of adult behavior that drives teenagers insane.

Rotten start to what will probably be a rotten day.

* * *

Hung out at Virgin Megastore listening to tunes all day. Didn't buy a thing except for a Coke I drank while waiting for the bus.

Just heard Crappy choking in the hallway and went to see if he was dying, and there was Cory, who pretended not to see me as she squatted down to pet Crappy. Only, she calls him Mozart. I figured it was a chance to talk, so I said, "Sounds like he swallowed a sponge or something." She didn't look up. She just said, "I can't hear a word you're saying," then picked up Crappy and took him into her room.

At least we spoke. It's a start.

twenty-seven

Leila called last night before I went to bed and said she'd just gotten home. She couldn't talk because she had things to do, but we made plans to meet on the steps of the library today. It made me feel good that she called me first thing. That's what you do when you miss somebody.

That was last night, before we met this afternoon and talked.

Now I'm not sure how I feel.

The thing is, Leila loved the farm she stayed on and the people who own it. Fine. But she also met a student-exchange guy from Germany who was staying on a neighbor's farm, and I got a funny feeling about him.

She actually sighed when she told me his name is Sebastian.

I've known Leila a long time and she's not the sighing type, so something is up. She has also known me a long time, and I must have looked morose while she was telling me about him, because she leaned against me and said, "It's okay for me to make friends, isn't it?"

I forced a smile and told Leila of course she could make all the friends she wants, then added that I was happy for her. My voice must not have been very convincing when I said that, because she said, "You don't sound happy, Max. It's okay if you're not. I'll understand."

I muttered something lame like "Naw. I'm really happy. You met a guy. That's great."

The thing that got me most is, Sebastian is coming to New York tomorrow and staying at Leila's place, which is so tiny she calls it a shoe box. I guess it makes sense he can't afford a hotel for three nights, which is how long he's supposed to stay, but I can't imagine where Leila will put him. Maybe a cot in the kitchen.

What confuses me is the way Leila said she wanted

me to meet Sebastian, and for us to hang together. She sounded sincere about that, so maybe he's not real boyfriend material. Anyway, I told her to call when she had a plan and maybe I'd meet them somewhere.

After that awkward part of our conversation was done, we hung on the library steps and analyzed faces for a couple of hours. It reminded me that no matter what, Leila is my friend.

twenty-eight

Leila's friend arrived this afternoon. I know because she called when they got back to her place after dinner. I didn't ask where they ate. I didn't care. She wanted to know if I'd meet them on the street by the Empire State Building tomorrow at eleven. I said, "Yeah, sure. I'll be there."

I think Leila was annoyed by my lack of enthusiasm. She'll get over it.

Nothing more to say tonight.

twenty-nine

Interesting day. On the ride downtown I told myself not to have a bad attitude, because people from Europe already think Americans are jerks, and I didn't want to be an example of that.

It turned out that Sebastian is a pretty cool guy. He has blond dreadlocks and had on jeans with the knees worn out, speaks pretty good English for a foreigner, and seemed real pleased to meet me. I almost hate to admit it, but I liked the guy.

It cost sixteen dollars to ride to the top of the Empire State Building. Rip-off. I wouldn't have gone if they weren't going, but there we were, and I didn't want to be a cheapskate, plus I hadn't been up since I was a squirt. So I paid and went, and was glad I did.

I think Leila might be a little afraid of heights, because after we got to the top she started talking about the difference between physical fears and phobias. She said physical fear was the body shooting out chemicals as a natural reaction to real danger, but a phobia was caused by unnatural chemicals manufactured in the brain. It was tricky grasping exactly what she meant, and I speak English, so I don't know how much Sebastian understood. He must have gotten the basics, though, because when Leila was done talking he told us about a nightmare he keeps having where he's on an airplane and gets up to go to the bathroom, then opens the door and accidentally steps into space. Said he could actually feel himself falling, and that's when he wakes up.

After we discussed Sebastian's nightmare for a few minutes, he and Leila looked at me like it was my turn to volunteer something. I just crossed my arms and didn't speak. It's good to be mysterious sometimes. For a couple of minutes there I actually felt back on my game.

Next we went for pizza at a deli, and Sebastian tried to pay for all of us. For some stupid reason, I told him to get Leila's if he wanted, but I insisted on paying for my own. He didn't argue.

We went from pizza to hang in Union Square, where Leila got on a roll making wicked remarks about the other people hanging out. At one point she had Sebastian and me laughing so hard we could hardly breathe. I think she enjoyed having two guys for an audience. Then, after an hour or so, she and Sebastian went to visit Ground Zero, and I headed back uptown, where I had bucketloads of nothing to do.

Now that I've met Sebastian, it doesn't bother me so much that Leila maybe found a boyfriend. I mean, if somebody besides me has to get lucky with Leila, it might as well be him. Besides, he may not get lucky. He's only here for three days, and I never saw them hold hands or anything. They could just be friends.

thirty

Woke up for no reason and looked at the clock. It was five to five. I couldn't sleep so I got out of my rectangular-shaped bed, walked down the hallway, went into the communal cube, and turned on the boob box. Soon as it flicked on, a man said, "This woman was locked in a basement for twenty years." It was all I needed to know. I turned off the box, came back to my box in a box, and wrote this in my square notebook.

What do you have when you put nothing in a box? Square nothing.

Bored, bored, bored, bored, bored. Like counting sheep.

thirty-one

Mom called for me to come into the kitchen about ten o'clock this morning, and I could tell from her voice that it was important. I went, and there was Crappy, dead on the floor beside the litter box. It finally happened.

The amazing thing was, there was a fresh turd lying perfectly in the middle of the box.

I looked at the turd and looked at Crappy, then looked at Mom, who said, "It's been months since I changed his box. This was the first time he used it."

"That must've been what killed him," I told Mom. "Poor cat. He probably knew the litter box was dangerous all along."

Mom sighed and reminded me that Aunt Ginny had given us Mozart when I was two. No one said anything for a minute. I was upset, but not too much. I asked Mom what we were going to do with the body. She didn't know. She said she wished Dad was home, but he'd left early in the morning for Toronto to shoot his headache commercial. Cory wasn't home either, so it was up to Mom and me to decide something.

We considered the logical stuff, like calling a vet or a pet funeral service, or putting him in a bag and me taking him to Central Park, but we didn't like any of those ideas. Finally, Mom pointed out that Cory was closer to Mozart than anyone and said we should wait for her to come home on lunch break—see if she had any ideas. I said that was fine, but should we just leave Mozart on the floor for two hours? I never use his other name in front of Mom. She doesn't approve. Anyhow, she said, "I don't know, Max. He looks so peaceful where he is."

I couldn't help myself. I burst out laughing and said, "That's not peace, Mom. It's death."

Mom couldn't help herself. We both stood there

laughing at Mozart. Anyone watching through a window would have thought we were crazy. We aren't. It was just a strangely funny moment, that's all.

I wrote the above several hours ago, before Cory came home for lunch. I stayed in my room when I heard her come in. Mom thought it was better if she informed Cory about Mozart—not me—and I agreed.

Curiosity got me after they'd been alone in the kitchen for like ten minutes, so I went to see what was happening. Mom was on the phone and Cory was kneeling on the floor, wrapping Mozart in aluminum foil. They'd come up with a plan and were putting it into action, although I wasn't sure what it was. At first when I asked, nobody answered, but then I heard Mom saying into the phone, "We're putting him in the freezer now. He should be all right there until we decide how to deliver him." There was a pause while Mom listened and Cory finished wrapping Crappy, then Mom said, "Excellent idea, Ginny. I'll speak with Max and call you tonight."

The upshot is, I'm leaving on a bus tomorrow for

Woodstock, New York. I'll be taking extra clothes, some money, my notebook, and one frozen, dead, aluminum-foiled cat. Crappy is going to be buried behind Aunt Ginny's barn, in a grave beside his sister, Madame Chow.

That's life. I was looking for something to do and something found me. Should be an interesting trip.

One benefit of Crappy dying is that Cory and I are on talking terms again. I caught her sobbing in the living room this evening and said real sweetly, "Don't cry, Cory. He lived a good life." She boo-hooed at that, and I was afraid I'd only made things worse, so I tried to fix it by adding, "It's not worth crying over. Pets die every day."

Then she looked up at me and blurted, "I'm not crying about Mozart, you nitwit. I'm crying because Ryan Cortland dumped me."

I said I didn't know they were a couple, and Cory explained they hadn't been, formally, but he'd been acting like he was going to ask her to go steady. It seemed obvious to me that if they weren't going steady, he couldn't dump her, but I didn't point that out to Cory. Instead I offered to find him and beat him to a pulp, and Cory sort of cry-laughed and said, "I bet you would."

Anyhow, I'm glad we had our conversation. Now I can go away without wondering if my own sister will ever speak to me again.

thirty-two

The Pine Hill bus is pulling out of Port Authority now. It's supposed to get to Woodstock at quarter to twelve. I would've taken the train, but then Aunt Ginny would have to drive to Poughkeepsie to pick me up, and Mom said it was too much to ask.

The bus is not bad. Crappy and I have seats to ourselves.

Actually, he's in a gym bag in the overhead rack. I told him to behave.

Being from New York, I'm used to seeing unusual people. Still, it seems like a lot of individualists got on this bus. It may be my imagination. I haven't traveled anywhere lately.

One old guy in the window seat across the aisle has a

long, white ponytail and is wearing John Lennon glasses. He nodded to me when he got on. I would talk to him if a woman hadn't taken the seat between us. If she wasn't there, I'd lean over and say, "Hello, Grandpa Hippie. What's happening?"

It surprised me how sad Leila got when I called last night to tell her Crappy died. She said us chasing Mozart through the halls of our building was one of her best childhood memories. It's funny what people remember. When I told her I was taking Crappy to be buried upstate and might be gone a week, she said send her a postcard, please. Sebastian must've been sitting in her lap listening, because I heard his voice, and then Leila said, "You're invited to stay at Sebastian's any time you want to go to Germany." Right. Like I can afford a trip to Europe.

Trevor was flat on the phone when I called him. It seemed he couldn't be bothered with news of someone else's dead pet. I got a little ticked off and asked him, "Where's your Buddhist compassion?" But the only answer he could think of was, "Sorry, Max."

He better snap out of it soon. It's getting harder and harder for me to remember why we're friends.

The woman in the next seat over got off the bus in New Paltz, and I had a talk with the old hippie. His name is Allen August. He's in the bathroom now. Our conversation started when he said he'd noticed me writing and asked if I was a poet. I said, "Nope. I'm a philosopher." He said, "I'm impressed." Then I asked if he had any poems published, and he told me no, but he was probably the best, most eloquent unpublished poet on our bus. Here he comes.

We're pulling into Woodstock now.

PART TWO

Upstate

thirty-three

Crappy must have thawed out a little bit on the ride, because the bottom of the gym bag was damp when I got off the bus. That freaked out Aunt Ginny, who drove like mad to her place and started me digging a hole before I even got my stuff out of the car.

We gave Crappy a simple funeral. Basically, I dug a hole beside Madame Chow's grave, took Crappy out of the gym bag, removed all the aluminum foil, and stuck him in the ground. I have to give Cory credit. She had done an excellent job wrapping the devil. His fur was sticky and one of his eyes sort of bulged out of his head. Otherwise he looked pretty good. Anyhow, Aunt Ginny chanted while

I was covering Crappy with dirt. Then we put a rock over his head and that was that.

I like the way Aunt Ginny fixed up her place. It's basically an old barn with new floors and plumbing, and windows and a kitchen and stuff. Everything is in one huge room, except the bathroom and her bedroom. The big room is so big you could move furniture and play putt-putt golf. I'm staying in what's called the summer room. It's a screened-in porch with a couch, a table, and some chairs.

Good thing I'm not afraid of the woods, because the trees come so close to the porch I could open the screen door and pee on one. I've never lived in the woods before. I've never even lived on the ground floor.

Right around sunset, the frogs in the marsh behind the barn go crazy croaking and don't stop until an hour or two after dark. Then it gets spooky quiet around here. I've never heard so much silence. Nothing honks or bangs or hums. Nothing. It's hard for me to sleep, which is why I'm up writing at midnight.

Wait. There's a dog barking in the distance. That's better.

thirty-four

Great. I've been here a day a half and have so many mosquito bites I look like I have measles. Got them on my hands, arms, legs, back, neck, and my face. There's an itchy spot on my ear, too, but I think that's poison ivy.

What happened was, when the frogs in the marsh went berserk this evening, I went out to see if I could see one. Sounded like a million of them out there, and I figured I couldn't miss. I still can't believe I didn't see a frog, but I didn't. Anyway, I was in the marsh, bending over looking under some ferns, when a giant cloud of mosquitoes appeared out of nowhere and attacked. Vicious little suckers. They'd have eaten me alive if I hadn't run like hell back to the barn.

I'm trying not to scratch my face. It reminds me too much of Trevor, just before he went over the edge.

The quiet is keeping me awake again. I'm hungry and would go fix something to eat, but all Aunt Ginny has in her kitchen is health-food crap. I told her today if she wanted me to stay longer like she said she wanted me to, then we had to make a grocery run. She told me we'd go first thing tomorrow morning.

Guess I'll eat an apple. Keep from starving.

I was in the kitchen looking for peanut butter to go on my apple when Aunt Ginny called from her bedroom, "Max, is that you?"

I said, "No. It's Donald Trump. Got any peanut butter?"

She said, "In the fridge."

I looked and saw the peanut butter, but I left it because I hate cold peanut butter. After I turned off the light in the kitchen and was coming back to my room, Aunt Ginny hollered that it felt good having a man around the house, and she was glad I was here.

"I'm glad too," I called back. That might be true.

thirty-five

Aunt Ginny took me grocery shopping early this morning because she had to go and come back, then drive back to town in time for her big Saturday yoga class. I had money Mom gave me for buying food, but I didn't get all the things I wanted because Aunt Ginny frowned every time I picked up what she thought was junk, which was almost everything in the store.

I'm on the deck now. It's noon and I've been alone for more than three hours. No one in the city is ever totally alone. There is always someone behind you, beside you, or in the next room, or whatever. When you're alone in the country, though, you can scream bloody murder and no one hears you.

BLOODY MURDER!

Yep, no one heard me. It's a fact.

It's strange when you're alone and the only thing happening is what's happening in your head. Aunt Ginny says positive thinking can do miracles. Okay. I'll give it a shot.

Max Whooten is handsome and smart and has just been having bad luck finding a girlfriend. He deserves the best. Any minute now a bunch of beautiful girls are going to walk out of the woods and dance naked in the yard.

Waiting.

Still waiting.

Yeah, right. So much for positive thinking.

A normal person in my situation would probably read a book, but I didn't bring one, and all Aunt Ginny has are for New Age, vegetarian, yoga instructors. Oh well. I'm not normal anyway.

Is anybody normal?

"How ya doing?"

"I'm average. How you doing?"

"I'm regular."

"Glad to hear it."

Found an exercise trampoline under the deck, dragged it into the yard and bounced up and down until I got bored. Then I did twenty push-ups and fifty jumping jacks.

That guy Allen on the bus was interesting. I don't meet a lot of old people I like, but I liked him. It was funny, him saying he was the best unpublished poet on the bus.

Maybe those naked girls took a wrong turn somewhere. Either that or the mosquitoes drove them off.

thirty-six

Aunt Ginny found me sleeping on the deck when she got home this afternoon. I wasn't wearing a shirt, and now I'm so sunburned I can't lie on my back. Basically, I've turned into one large, pink, fried mosquito bite.

Spoke with Mom and Dad tonight. He got back from Toronto this morning. Said the commercial went fine. Both he and Mom encouraged me to stay with Aunt Ginny as long as I was comfortable. They said things like it was good for her to have company; the country air would do me some good; and it was hot in the city. It was pretty obvious they didn't want me home.

Fine. I'll hang here a few days. Let Cory and the P's have the Whooten Box to themselves.

I felt like I was on fire from head to toe a little while ago, so Aunt Ginny put aloe vera on my back. Cooled me down pretty good. I guess some New Age stuff really does work. Tomorrow is Sunday, and she offered to show me around Woodstock. I told her just to show me the shady spots.

I'm kind of excited about seeing Woodstock, despite Dad saying it had gone from being a funky little hippie village to a trendy destination for SUV-driving posers who wash with French soap. He can be pretty cynical sometimes. It's one thing I like about him.

Anyhow, Woodstock is famous because of a movie they made about a festival that took place near there a long time ago. The festival became famous after a huge crowd of people listened to music in the rain for three days and nobody had a fight. I've seen the movie twice and would watch it again just to see Jimi Hendrix.

* * *

"Excuse me while I kiss the sky."

Jimi Hendrix

Hear that dog in the distance again. It sounds worried about something.

thirty-seven

Aunt Ginny and I had brunch and walked around Woodstock for a couple of hours today. It's not very big, but I thought it was sort of cool. I told her what Dad said about it being a place for people who bathe with French soap, and she said maybe for once Dad wasn't all wrong.

It seemed Aunt Ginny knew everybody in town, which is okay unless you're trying to get somewhere in a hurry. I bet we stopped and talked to thirty people. Most of her friends were vegetarian yoga women like her, but a few were guys. One in particular laid a real flirt on Aunt Ginny, and she didn't seem to mind. I think his name was Reginald. I was happy to see her getting action, but it was a little weird for me to watch. I mean, I know old people do stuff. I just don't like being reminded of the fact.

Bought a postcard of a cow smoking a pipe to send to Leila.

Aunt Ginny and I bumped into Allen August when we were getting in the car to come home. She was surprised after he said howdy to her, then stuck out his hand to me and said, "How's it going, Max?"

I told him everything was fine as long as no one slapped my back, because I had a sunburn.

He said I did look radioactive.

Allen could see we were just getting in the car to go, so he said, "Look, I won't keep you talking, but if either of you is interested in hearing me read some new poems, I'm featured at the Colony tomorrow night. Starts at seven." When I told him I might come, he said, "Hope you do. I'd be proud to have a philosopher in the audience."

On the ride home Aunt Ginny offered to drop me at

the Colony tomorrow night, then come back and pick me up later. She said she wasn't interested in going because she's heard Allen read his poems before, and once was enough. Plus she has a pregnant women yoga class on Monday nights. I asked was that safe, pregnant women doing pretzels and headstands. She laughed and said it was mostly a stretching and breathing class.

It's obvious Aunt Ginny wants me to feel comfortable here, because she made a pizza for dinner tonight and served ice cream for dessert. After that we had tea and sat around talking for hours. There was nothing else to do. The woman doesn't even own a TV.

I forget how we got on the subject, but we spent a lot of time discussing my life. She said I seemed much mellower now than when we talked at the start of the summer. I agreed that might be true and gave her credit for getting me to write, then told her about the day in the library when I decided to quit thinking so much about stuff and just cool out. First she said, "I thought your generation said chill instead of cool," and I said, "A lot of them do, but not me." Then she told me it sounded like I'd had an epiphany in the library. I said, "Maybe. I don't know. What's an epiphany?" and she explained that an epiphany was a sudden, clear understanding of a situation.

Interesting. I had an epiphany. It didn't hurt at all.

thirty-eight

I went last night to Phillip's Open Mic Monday Night Poetry Reading Forever. That's what the thing at the Colony Cafe is called. The three dollars for getting in is called a donation so people feel better about paying.

Except for me and one girl sitting by herself in the balcony, everyone there was over forty or fifty. I don't hold being old against anybody, but it's obvious age affects the kind of poems people write. The older the poet is, the more they seem to want to be shocking.

I'm not a trained critic, but Leila's poems are a lot better than most of the ones I heard last night. Allen was good at reading aloud. The main problem with his poems, though, is they're too long and too complicated to follow. Still, he was the most interesting poet there. One guy was so bad, people booed to get him to stop, but he didn't. He went on and on and on. Listening to him was sort of like sitting in the waiting room for hell.

That girl in the balcony was cute. I went up to the bathroom once and got a good look at her from the side. She was drawing in a sketch pad and pretended not to see me, but I know she did. I saw her turn away when I came out the door. Maybe she's shy.

Allen saw me in the crowd and nodded hello when he went up to read, but we never got a chance to talk because he was surrounded by people at the end, and I left as soon as Aunt Ginny got there.

Here's an idea for a poem. It's sort of about how I feel and sort of just an idea.

> *i have a friend*
> *she's really wow*
> *went away to see a cow*
> *met some guy*
> *i don't know how*
> *kissing me she won't allow*

oou ouch ow
my fuse is lit
i'm exploding now

Poetry is not too hard. All you need is a pen, some paper, some feelings, and a few ideas.

Aunt Ginny showed me the shelf in her bedroom where she keeps her novels, in case I have a normal fit and want to read. I found one by Kurt Vonnegut that looks interesting. Maybe I'll start that tomorrow.

thirty-nine

Today is Wednesday the twenty-seventh, which means
Cory turns fifteen in three days. Most of the time I'm two
years older than she is, but every year between the thirti-
eth of July and the twenty-second of August I'm only one
year older. When we were kids I used to act worried that
she was catching up with me.

Aunt Ginny has told me so many times to feel free to
use the phone, she's practically been begging, so tonight
I did her a favor and made some calls.

I had the idea of calling Cory and telling her I
wouldn't be there for her birthday, then taking the bus
home and surprising her. But when I called the box, Mom

told me Cory had taken a week off from work and gone to Cape Cod with the DePrees. Great. My little sister is hanging with her rich friend at the beach while I'm stuck in mosquitoville with my lonely, vegetarian aunt.

It gets worse. When I asked Mom how she and Dad were doing, she got really excited and said this was the first week they would be spending alone since either of them could remember, and they had a couple of dates planned. I'm not a baby. I didn't make a fuss about everybody in my family having fun but me. Then Mom asked how I was, and I said, "Terrific. Getting plenty of rest," and we hung up. It was weird. My own mother didn't even ask when I was coming home.

I called Leila and got her address. She said I was lucky to catch her because she'd just walked in the door. It was ten thirty at night, so I asked where she'd been. First she told me I was starting to sound like her mom. Then she said she got a job at a clothing store on Avenue A, and they didn't close until ten. I told her I didn't even know she was looking for a job. She said she got the idea yesterday, and the second place she went hired her to work the register, which was easy because it's a designer store that doesn't sell much.

So . . . Leila snaps her fingers and gets a job. I didn't say it, but one of the benefits of being a beautiful chick in the city is getting what you want.

Anyhow, the real truth came out when I asked Leila how things went with Sebastian. She said wonderful, part of why she got a job was to maybe earn some money for a trip to Germany. I had a rotten reaction to that and almost said something rude, but I caught myself and told her instead, "Good for you. I have to go now. Aunt Ginny doesn't like me using her phone."

Get back on your game, Max. Don't be lame. Don't go insane.

Philosophical question: Is life supposed to be a confused mess that even people who have had an epiphany cannot understand?

forty

It's hard to believe, but I think I met a girl I like who actually likes me. It's the girl from the poetry reading. She's sixteen, and her name is Zini. She's short, has dark eyes, and curly brown hair that she lets grow out of control.

Zini is an artist and can draw people who look like real people with real emotions. You have to be sensitive and smart to do that. I can't remember meeting anybody more interesting to watch when she talks.

I met Zini today when Aunt Ginny dropped me off at the post office while she ran errands in town. It only took me five minutes to buy a stamp and mail Leila's card. Then

I went to wait on the Green, where Aunt Ginny said she'd pick me up in an hour. The Green is a park about the size of a basketball court. I had *God Bless You, Mr. Rosewater* by Kurt Vonnegut with me and sat down to read while I waited, although I couldn't concentrate because there were goths on one of the other benches, and just being near them freaked me out. I've seen plenty of goths before, but this bunch was seriously insane, which I think is their point. Anyhow, I sort of pretended to read and kept one eye on the goths in case they decided to do something crazy, and didn't notice at first that a girl had walked over to my bench, until she said, "Mind if I sit here?" I looked up, and there was Zini holding a sketch pad. I told her, "It's fine with me. Go ahead. Sit."

I hate being shy. It's ridiculous. I wanted to say something, but didn't know what to say. Plus, I know sometimes girls want to be left alone, and get mad if guys hassle them, but sometimes they get mad at guys who won't make a move. So I never know what to do, and we both sat there. Finally, Zini sort of giggled and asked, "Are you blushing?"

I told her, "No. I have a sunburn. It was worse before."

Then she said, "Oh," and I said, "Hi. My name is Max. I think I saw you the other night at the poetry thing."

She started flipping through her pad and didn't say anything, and I figured she didn't want to talk. But I was wrong. Because then she found what she was looking for, handed me her pad, and said, "I saw you too."

Talk about feeling terrific. She'd done a drawing of me leaning over the table with my head in my hands. It was mostly a top view, so you couldn't see my face, but you could tell from the way she drew me that I was bored. I told her, "That's great. Really great." Then she thanked me for the compliment and we were off to the races talking.

First she told me her name was Zini Cabrini and she'd just moved to Woodstock from Vermont three weeks ago. Then I told her I was from the city and had come to Woodstock to bury a cat. Zini got a concerned look on her face and asked was the cat dead. I said of course it was dead. Then she asked was it my cat or one I found somewhere, and I suddenly realized she was joking. She has a bent sense of humor. I like that in a girl.

After that we talked nonstop until Aunt Ginny tooted

her horn for me to come. Zini cracked me up most of the time. One hilarious thing she said was when I asked if Zini was her real first name. She pretended to be offended by the question and said, "We just met, Max. What kind of girl do you think I am?"

I said, "Sorry if I was rude."

She sort of smiled with her eyes and said, "Zini rhymes with teeny. It's a nickname. I used to be very small."

I'm out of practice feeling happy like this, so it's hard to trust my own thinking, but the more I remember being with Zini today, the more I think a miracle happened.

My only mistake was forgetting to ask when I could see her again.

forty-one

I really might be cursed, or I'm an idiot. I guess I hope I'm cursed.

I was scrambling eggs this morning and reached for salt on the shelf above the stove when my shirt caught fire. I smelled smoke before I saw the fire and reacted just in time to save my life, and Aunt Ginny's barn. She never would have forgiven me if I'd burned down her home.

Aunt Ginny had a lot of running around to do today, so I got her to draw me a map so I can walk to town and look for Zini. It's 1.4 miles. I know blocks better than miles, but I don't think that's far. I take two lefts and a right, then follow Rock City Road to the Green. No problem.

Two dogs nearly scared me to death when I was walking here, but I made it. Now I'm sitting on the bench where I met Zini, writing in my notebook. It was about one o'clock when we met yesterday. A couple of minutes ago I asked somebody with a watch what time it was, and she said twenty to one.

A guy just came over and asked for a dollar. I said, "Nope."

He said, "Please, man. I really need a dollar."

I gave him a quarter, for being polite.

Eliot Rosewater, the rich nutcase in the book I'm reading, would've probably given the guy a thousand dollars.

It must be one thirty by now. Come on, Miss Cabrini, I'll buy you a zucchini and a weeny beanie to wear on your head.

Max is a nice guy. He'd make a great boyfriend. Max deserves the best. He is the best.

Come on, Zini.

Just told some dude I didn't want to buy grass. First I tried saying I didn't have any money, but then he said he could break it up if I only wanted a little. I told him, "Forget it. I'm allergic to the stuff."

It's got to be three o'clock by now. I'm starting to feel more and more like an idiot for sitting here.

Girls. Can't count on them for nothing.

That's it. I'm going.

forty-two

Aunt Ginny is napping and I'm sitting on the deck wondering why nothing ever goes right for me. I waited four hours yesterday for Zini, but she never showed. Of course, we didn't have plans to meet or anything, but still, if she was interested she would've come. Unless she had plans.

Who knows? I don't.

I think it's time to head back to my box in the city, sit around and think square thoughts with the rest of the blockheaded people.

Almost forgot, today is Cory's fifteenth birthday. I bet she went to a fancy, oceanfront restaurant to eat lobster and flaming ice cream with her rich friends. Good for her.

At least my sunburn is fading into a nice tan.

Aunt Ginny wants me to go with her to a cookout this evening.

When she told me about it, I said I wasn't in the mood for meeting a bunch of New Age people. That ticked her off, and she said, "You can have the blues if you want, Max, but that doesn't give you the right to be rude to me or criticize the New Age. It may not be perfect, but it beats the hell out of the spiritually bankrupt society the old age has given us. Now quit moaning and take a shower. Like it or not, we're leaving here at six."

Aunt Ginny totally changes when she gets fired up. Reminds me of Dad.

Better go shower.

forty-three

I'm zooming. It's past midnight, but I feel too good to sleep. Zini Cabrini was at that cookout Aunt Ginny dragged me to tonight. It was a huge surprise. The cookout was way out in the sticks, and I never even hoped Zini would be there. She came because the woman who gave the party is a Pilates teacher, and Zini's mom signed up for the class right after they moved to Woodstock. Aunt Ginny likes the woman who gave the party, but she doesn't care much for Pilates. It cuts in on her yoga trade.

Anyways . . . I'm zooming, thanks to one cute, smart, sexy artist with curly brown hair.

I admit, I was in a crappy mood when Aunt Ginny and

I arrived at the cookout. The food was in the front yard and the drinks were in the side yard, and people were wandering in and out of the house and standing on the porch. Aunt Ginny walked me to the side yard and said, "You're on your own from here, Max. You can mope around all night if you want, but leave me out of it." I told her, "Don't worry. I'll mope quietly."

I got a soda and leaned against a tree at the edge of the yard. Everyone who glanced over turned away. I probably looked like a troubled teen, and no one likes them. It's not that people are afraid. They just don't want to get involved. It could be worse. At least I'm not a crackhead.

So I was just standing there being morose when Zini walked out of the house, saw me under the tree, waved, and came straight over. I could hardly believe it. She actually skipped on her way across the yard.

After we both said hi, Zini said, "I was hoping I'd see you again."

I said, "Really?"

And she said, "Of course, really."

Then I told her I waited four hours on the Green

yesterday hoping she'd come. She liked that. I could tell from her smile.

We talked a lot and it was a great night. Zini told me she and her parents had moved to Woodstock to live with her grandmother, who was getting too old to take care of herself. That was good because her parents got to sell their place in Burlington and keep the money, and that took pressure off her dad, who is an illustrator. I told Zini it sounded like my situation, except my dad was an actor and we weren't moving. She said, "Wow. One out of three similarities. We're practically identical." Her mind is quick like that.

Zini has never been to New York City, and I told her any time she wants to visit, I'd take her places. I also said it was a good idea for girl visitors to walk around with a guy, because of the creeps. She opened her eyes real wide when I said that and told me I was gallant. It's not always obvious when Zini is joking. I think she might have been teasing me. So what.

Later we sat on the porch and she talked about her

friends that she misses in Vermont. She mentioned some guys but didn't say anything about a boyfriend. One of her friends named Bella might visit next week. I told her about Trevor losing the plot and about Leila being a great poet, and this notebook I'm writing, and said I had a sister named Cory. Zini said she was jealous because she'd always wanted a brother or sister. I told her she could have Cory, and she said, "When can I pick her up?"

Then Zini grabbed my hand and tugged me down the steps and across the yard to meet her parents. At first I thought she was being romantic, then I realized she just didn't want me to escape. Still, we held hands.

Her dad has long hair on the sides of his head but is bald on top. Her mom is small and her hair is almost as curly as Zini's. Anyway, when she introduced me, her mom said, "You must be the cat undertaker from New York City." I blushed, but it was dark and didn't matter. I was happy knowing that Zini had talked about me.

A few minutes after that I introduced Zini to Aunt Ginny. They clicked straight off and found like five things to laugh about in three minutes of talking.

Zini and I hugged good-bye at the end when everybody started leaving. There were people standing around so we didn't kiss, but I got a feeling it was something we might do soon. Maybe tomorrow, which is actually today since it's quarter past one. We're meeting on the Green at noon. That's less than eleven hours from now, more or less.

On the ride home tonight Aunt Ginny told me she was impressed with Zini, and I said, "You're impressed? I'm astonished."

I am astonished. I found a girlfriend, maybe.

Still zooming. Probably lie awake all night.

forty-four

Everything I'd been hoping would happen is happening. It's frightening. I'm not used to life going great.

There's a creek called Tannery Brook that runs through the middle of Woodstock. Zini and I took off our shoes and followed it today until we found some rocks for sitting in the sun. She had her pad and drew an interesting picture of our bare feet sticking in the water. I asked if she'd sign it and give it to me, and she said, "Sure, since you're letting me read your notebook." When I told her I hadn't agreed to that, she stared hard at me and said, "What are you afraid I'll find out?"

Finally I said, "Okay. You can pick a page and read it." She said, "I'll only read three. Or four."

I don't know which pages she read because she told me to give her some space while she read, but when she was done she handed me my notebook and said, "Interesting."

I asked, "What do you mean, 'interesting'?"

And she said, "Interesting means interesting."

I told her I knew what the word means, it was the way she used it I was curious about.

She looked into the water and said, "It's interesting because now I know more about you and your life, and your friend Leila. You like her a lot, don't you?"

I said, "Leila and I have been friends forever. I told you that."

Zini just nodded and kept looking in the water. So I asked her what she was thinking, and she said, "Just life."

It was kind of a strange moment. We were both quiet for a long time.

Later I walked Zini to the gate in front of her grand-mother's house at the edge of town. We sort of hesitated there, and I was wondering if I should kiss her good-bye or just hug her like we'd done before, when she stuck out her hand, which I took to shake. Then she raised up on her toes and pecked me on my cheek. It was a long way from making out, but it was something. After she went through the gate, she turned and called, "Now that you know where I live, Max, you're welcome to stop by."

I said, "Great. Tell me when?"

And she said, "Tomorrow around noon, if you want."

When I was walking away I was thinking: If you want? What kind of question is that?

Of course I want.

forty-five

I'm on the deck, getting ready to go see Zini. Before I go, I'm writing down the weird dream I had last night.

Zini and I were standing on Broadway, holding hands and waiting for the light to change, when Toshen Chenault came over. He was with some girl. I didn't recognize her until she said, "How was Brazil?" Then I saw it was Iris from the dance studio. At the same time, Toshen noticed Zini, and I said, "I bought her chocolate." Then Iris pulled out a camera and took a picture of Zini, except Zini turned into Leila and walked into traffic. So I went to get her, and she was Zini, only not exactly. After that I woke up.

I don't know what a dream expert would say my dream

meant, but it reminded me to buy Zini some chocolate. It also reminded me to triple-brush my teeth and gargle . . . just in case she leans over and bats her eyelashes and says, "Kiss me, Max."

Zini and I are sitting in the sun on the rock we found the other day. She's drawing clouds now and I'm writing in my notebook. She's wearing a blue jean skirt that almost disappears underneath her on the rock. She has nice legs. On top she's wearing a T-shirt and a bra that I can see when she angles her arm just right.

I don't think peeking at her bra makes me a pervert.

Probably should have stopped on my way here and bought chocolate. This would be the perfect time to give it to her.

I have to be careful what I write, in case Zini tries to read this later, but I feel like putting my notebook down, grabbing her around the waist, and kissing her until she faints.

And when she faints, I'll dip her in the creek and bring her back to consciousness.

Then we'll splash around in the water and kiss some more.

If anyone named Zini reads this, Max is just kidding.

Zini is still drawing clouds. It feels like she's ignoring me, but I know she's just concentrating. Art is important to Zini. By the way, her real first name is Marie. I heard her grandmother call her that before we left the house, but I pretended I didn't hear. So did Zini.

It's Monday, August first. I'll be seventeen in twenty-one days. I'm taking driver's ed this fall. It'll be cool, having a license, although I don't have a car and neither does Mom or Dad. Just have to rent one when I want to go places, like Woodstock on the weekends. Or out to Colorado. Or down to Brazil.

forty-six

Not a good morning.

Yesterday I gave Aunt Ginny's number to Zini, in case she wanted to talk. She called this morning, and Aunt Ginny answered, and when I walked into the big room I heard her saying, "The four o'clock on Tuesdays and Thursdays would be fine. Yes. Thrilled to have you. Tinker Street, that's right. Hold on. Here he is now."

I took the phone and said hello, and Zini said, "Hi, Max." Something in her voice clued me she didn't have good news. She didn't have bad news, exactly. It was just that she would be busy with her mom all day and didn't have time to hang out.

Maybe I overreacted. I was sort of joking, but it didn't come out funny. What I said was, "So you're ditching me?"

Zini sighed like she didn't have the patience for dealing with me and said, "What did I just tell you?"

I got her point, but I didn't act like I got it. I said, "You said you'd rather spend the day with your mom than me."

There was a long silence on the phone, after which Zini said, "Max. Listen to yourself."

I did, and didn't like what I heard, and said, "Sorry, Zini. I'm disappointed I won't be seeing you, that's all."

Then Zini said she was sorry she'd disappointed me, and we agreed to meet on the Green tomorrow.

After we hung up, Aunt Ginny said Zini had a special energy. For some reason it rubbed me wrong and I told her, "I bet everybody who takes one of your classes is special."

Aunt Ginny glared hard at me when I said that. I could almost hear her thinking: *Don't be childish, Max.*

Sometimes I act immature when I'm disappointed. I admit that. Zini can take any class she wants, and Aunt Ginny was just doing her thing. I feel like a jerk for having any feelings to begin with.

* * *

Stop, Max. You're doing it again. It's not even ten thirty and you're worked up over nothing.

Cool out.

Take a walk.

forty-seven

Today I followed a deer trail that Aunt Ginny had showed me behind the barn. Stupid me. I got the idea and took off without wearing socks or changing into long pants or leaving a note or taking a bottle of water or anything. I just figured I'd go a ways, then turn around and come back when I was ready. Only problem was the trail divided behind the marsh, then divided again in the woods, and finally faded into nothing. But I didn't care. I was thinking about Zini, and Leila and Sebastian, and Cory not talking to me, and just kept walking.

I have a pretty good sense of direction in the city, but not in the woods, where all you can see is bushes and trees, and so Max Whooten, the lucky genius from the Upper

West Side of New York City, got lost. I hate getting lost. Makes me feel like a moron, and no one thinks straight when they feel that way.

I don't know how long I zigzagged around before I sort of gave up and sat down. Probably a couple of hours, although it felt much longer. Long enough to worry I might have to spend the night in the woods and maybe a bear would eat me. I didn't really believe that, I don't think, but I imagined I did, and then I started wondering what if I died?

Interesting question. It really brought out the philosopher in me. After a while I thought, I haven't had sex yet. I'm too young to die. That put me back on my feet and walking again.

I can laugh about it now, because ten minutes after thinking I might die, I came out on the paved road near the turnoff to Aunt Ginny's barn.

Now I've eaten and had a shower and am sitting on the porch wondering what's happening with Zini and thinking I should buy her a box of chocolate and apologize for acting like an immature jerk on the phone.

forty-eight

Walked into Woodstock and bought eight dollars' worth of the best chocolate they had at the Candy and Fudge Store. It wasn't much, but the woman in the store wrapped it in pretty paper, and it looked okay for a gift.

Then I went and waited for Zini on the Green, and when she came I apologized for being weird on the phone with her. She told me not to worry about it, that one of the things she liked about me was I didn't hide my feelings, even when they weren't pleasant.

After that, she basically dumped me. Her excuse was she's worried about starting school in three weeks and not knowing any locals, and her friend Bella is coming from

Vermont the day after tomorrow, and she needed a break.

I almost exploded when I heard that, and I think my voice sounded rougher than I meant when I said, "A break from what? Me?"

She said, "You'll be leaving in a few days anyway, Max. You don't live here. Remember?"

I told her that was true, but New York wasn't so far away that I couldn't visit a lot.

And she said, "I hope you do, and I want to see you when you visit. I'm just going through a lot of adjustments right now and don't want to get confused. You know how that goes. You wrote about it in your notebook."

Here comes the crazy part. I asked Zini what pages she read in my notebook, and instead of answering my question, she asked, "Have you considered that maybe you're in love with Leila?"

I made a face like that wasn't even worth thinking about and didn't say anything. And Zini made a face like I was missing her whole point. Then I asked her, "So is that what you thought was interesting the other day? Reading about Leila?"

Zini nodded. "That's what was there."

I'm kind of proud of what I did next. Instead of blowing up like I felt like doing, I told myself to cool out, and did, and said, "Look. It's not what I want, but if you need a break, let's take one."

Zini stood up, pecked me on the cheek, and said, "Thanks for understanding, Max. That's what I hoped you'd do. I'll call you soon. Or you call me."

Then I just sat watching Zini walk away and didn't remember the chocolate in my bag until she was gone.

Now I know how Cory must've felt being dumped by someone she wasn't actually going with. Cory likes chocolate. Maybe I'll give what I bought to her.

On my way out of town I ran into Allen August, and he asked what I thought of his poetry the other night. I said it was pretty damn good. I couldn't bring myself to tell him the truth.

PART THREE

The City Again

forty-nine

It's been two days since Zini left me sitting on the Green.
She never called, so I called her this morning, but she
couldn't talk long because her friend Bella was there from
Vermont. So we basically just said good-bye. Then this
afternoon I took a bus back to the city.

You gotta love New York. First thing I saw when I
walked out of Port Authority was a guy puking on the
sidewalk. Then a fire engine got stuck in traffic right
where I was trying to cross the street, and nearly blasted
my ears off with its horn. The noise made me jump back,
and I almost landed on an old Hispanic woman's foot. She
just looked at me and shook her head.

The fire engine reminded me of Eliot Rosewater, the main character in the book I finished reading on the bus. He inherited eighty-four-million-and-something dollars, yet all he wanted to do was be a volunteer fireman and ride on fire engines. Problem was, the people in his world wouldn't accept him being a fireman, and that made him so depressed he went crazy.

They say writers should write about what they know. That Vonnegut guy who wrote about Eliot obviously knows a lot about insanity.

When I got home this afternoon, Dad said, "There you are, Max. It hasn't been the same around here without you." It was his way of welcoming me back to the Whooten Box.

Now I'm in my little box inside the boxes that make up the Whooten Box, and instead of a dog barking in the distance, I hear a car alarm and a siren. There are not enough places to put things in my box, so stuff is piled on stuff, and it looks like a mess. It is a mess, but I don't care. It's home.

* * *

The summer is slipping away. Starting right now I'm going to stay cooled out and not let stupid crap put me off my game.

Starting right now it's the new Max.

fifty

Trevor called this morning and came over. I was surprised. He was such a wreck last time I saw him, he wasn't going anywhere. But he quit his medicine a week ago and says he feels better than ever. He wasn't supposed to stop. He did it on his own.

He tried apologizing for slipping over the edge, but I told him there was nothing to be sorry about, I'd been kicking around the edge myself. He frowned at that and said we weren't talking about the same edge, the one he'd slipped over didn't have a bottom. He's right. I've been miserable a lot, but I always knew where the ground was. Anyhow, he seemed like he wanted to talk about what he'd been through, so I asked him what drove him over the edge. He said his parents, who were blind to who he really was. He'd gone to the edge trying to shake free of them and accidentally slipped. But it didn't matter now. He'd been to the bottom and back, and was ready to get on with his new life.

I asked Trevor if he was still going to be a Buddhist in his new life. He said, "Probably not. Buddhism taught me it was easier to be happy if you don't expect too much, and I'll keep that in mind, but I bumped into Macey Wyscoft two days ago and pretty much decided I'm not ready for the Golden Path."

When I reminded him he'd sworn he'd never be with Macey again, he said, "Yeah. Maybe I did. But that was before she burst out like a bomb."

I told Trevor, "Welcome back to the real world. I missed you." I meant it, too.

After that he asked me about Woodstock and I told him a little about meeting Zini, but then said I didn't want to talk about her. He said, "Why not?" and I said, "I just don't." Then he said, "Fine with me. I know all about not wanting to talk about things."

Yesterday I gave Cory the chocolate I bought for Zini, but I didn't tell her that, so Cory thought I bought it to make up for embarrassing her at Athena's party. She was really thankful and called me sweet. I said it was nothing and told her, "It didn't make sense to buy you flowers."

Then tonight Cory comes into my room and says she's buying a new laptop, and do I want her old desktop, which works great. Of course I said yes. Eight dollars' worth of chocolate for a computer. You can't beat that.

Leila is off from work tomorrow night, and we're having dinner together. She wants Indian food and offered to pay for us both. I said she didn't have to treat, but she said she definitely owed me for all the things I'd paid for in the past and don't argue, so I didn't. I also didn't mention that Indian food makes me burp.

Zini never called. How long is soon?

fifty-one

Yesterday, August ninth, was the best day I've had all summer. It started good before I even got out of bed. Dad came to my door and knocked, and instead of criticizing me for something, he said it wasn't a definite yet, but the art director of the movie he was in was looking for production assistants for several days before and after the week they film in Queens, and asked was I interested in working. I told him I was absolutely interested. Then he said he'd make a phone call and let me know.

I was getting dressed ten minutes later when Dad came back to my room and said I have to meet with a woman named Anne on Friday, and if I don't screw up the meeting, the job is mine.

Great. I'm not sure what a production assistant does or how much I'll get paid, but it's great.

When I thanked Dad for helping me, he said it was nothing, that most of the regular crew people they use are out of town at the end of August, and they're having a hard time finding help. Just show up on time and do what they tell me. And no sour grapes.

Dad likes saying no sour grapes. In my case it means no getting ticked off and quitting.

That was yesterday morning. Then last night I had dinner with Leila, and after I told her about me working on Dad's movie, she said she also had good news. The husband-and-wife designers who own the store where she works hired her to walk in two runway shows during fashion week this September. They aren't famous designers, and the shows will be in a downtown warehouse instead of in the tents behind Bryant Park, but Leila will get paid three hundred bucks per show, and that's just fine with her.

We both had to laugh at our good news. A month ago

we were impecunious nobodies. Now she's a model and I'm in the film biz.

I asked her if she was going to visit Sebastian in Germany with the money she earned. She said she thought Sebastian was sweet and she would like to see Europe one day, but going to Germany any time soon wasn't in the cards.

Have to admit I was happy to hear that.

Then Leila asked about my trip to Woodstock, and instead of beating around the bush, I told her straightaway about meeting Zini. That made Leila curious, as I knew it would, and she wanted to know all about Zini. For some reason, I didn't clam up with Leila like I did with Trevor, and pretty much told her everything, except the part where Zini wondered if I might be in love with Leila. There was no need to confuse things by mentioning that.

Leila listened real closely to every detail about Zini, then made me tell her twice about Zini dumping me. She kept shooting questions at me like I was in court or something. What did Zini say? What did you say? What did Zini say then? And so on.

Finally Leila had all the information she wanted and paused to think. After a couple of minutes she said, "You know I never tell you what to do, Max, but I'm telling you now. Buy another box of chocolates and send it to Zini with a letter saying you really dug meeting her and want to stay friends."

I just looked at Leila and shrugged.

Then she said, "This may come as a surprise to you, but girls are attracted to guys who can be friends."

"Oh?" I said. "Friends like us, you mean?"

Leila didn't answer my question. Instead she said, "Just send her chocolate and write an honest letter, and see what happens."

It just now hit me that girls are in a conspiracy together to get chocolate. They probably have codes only they understand. It wouldn't surprise me if after I send Zini the chocolate, she sends a few pieces to Leila as a kickback.

I better warn Toshen Chenault. He may not know what we're up against.

Maybe it didn't go the way I wanted with Zini, but at least something happened, which is better than the nothing that was going on in my life before we met.

fifty-two

I'm worried Trevor is getting better too fast. We hung out by the Columbus Circle entrance to Central Park today and he acted like some kind of sex maniac who'd never seen a pretty girl before.

Babe-watching is fine with me. I do it all the time. It was different with Trevor, though. Every other minute he'd jab me with an elbow and say things like, "Check her out, Max," or "I'd die to see her naked," or "Call a doctor," or "Man. She's on fire."

I finally told Trevor he was acting obsessed and to get a grip.

His reaction to that was, "What's wrong with being obsessed?"

I said, "Nothing, until you lose control of yourself and do something stupid."

He laughed at that and said, "Don't worry. I'm just looking. I'm not going to run out and tackle some chick."

I said I wasn't worried, I was just pointing out that last month he was on his way to being a Buddhist monk, and today he was behaving like a horny dog on steroids.

Trevor grew serious for a few seconds and thought about what I said. Then he said, "I know I have a problem with obsessions. It's who I am. I enjoy getting wrapped up in things."

I couldn't think of a comeback to that, so I didn't say anything.

Suddenly Trevor whistled real low under his breath and said, "Nine o'clock, Max. Brunette in microskirt."

What the hell? I turned to nine o'clock and looked. I have to admit, I was glad I did. Then I thought that guys sitting on benches watching girls walk by has been going on forever, and that the girls know they're being watched, and still they keep putting on microskirts and walking by.

When I pointed this out to Trevor, he said, "Why do you think man invented benches?"

Trevor's quick, except when he's completely out of his head. I suppose if he's going to go over the edge again, he might as well go for girls instead of some religion where you eat only one grain of rice a day.

Nothing against Buddha. Just making a comparison.

fifty-three

I had an interesting thought this morning when I was talking with Mom in the kitchen and she asked how my philosophy studies were going. I told her it was hard to measure because I'd had an epiphany and decided to invent my own branch. She looked like she didn't have a clue what I meant, so I told her, "You know. A philosophical branch." Then she nodded like she understood and asked what my branch was called. I hadn't thought about it before, but an idea popped into my head and I said, "Coolism. It's the philosophy of not thinking too much and just cooling out." I'm not sure if Mom followed what I was saying or not, but it all made sense to me.

Coolism. Sounds right. I like it.

Funny how life goes sometimes. I got dressed in my best jeans and a clean shirt, and was heading downtown on the subway for my interview about the production assistant job on Dad's movie, and was thinking about Coolism, when I noticed an idiot standing in the doorway so people could hardly get past him. Not only was he an idiot, but he smelled raunchy too, and when we stopped at Fifty-ninth he completely blocked a woman from getting off the train. She looked around like she was desperate for help, so I jumped over without thinking and shoved the guy out of the train with my foot. For a second or two I thought he was going to jump back in the car and and try to kick my ass, but some guys behind stepped forward like they were backing me up, and the idiot just stood there. Then the doors closed and the train took off, and then some people clapped like they thought I'd done a good thing. That made me feel great. It was sort of like having my hero dream, only better because it actually happened.

* * *

My meeting went well and I got the job. The pay is fantastic. One hundred and fifty dollars a day for four days. It's two days before they start filming and two after they're done. They'll be long days, but the work doesn't sound bad. Basically, I have to ride with a prop guy named Doug to pick up props in the city, drive to Queens, and help dress a house. Dress means decorate. I asked.

It's a dream gig. Six hundred dollars for two days on, three days off, and two days on. The only snag is, the day I start is my birthday. I'm not complaining, though. No sour grapes from me.

I never ever thought I'd say this, but I miss Crappy. The Whooten Box is different without him. It's hard to explain, but without Crappy, we seem like just another family living on the ninth floor of a square building on a square block. Plus, Crappy was perfect for when one of us wanted to complain about something but couldn't think of anything that was really wrong. We always had Crappy for that. Now we just have the news.

fifty-four

It's Saturday and I'm sitting in a coffee shop on Broadway writing in my notebook and drinking a very expensive milk shake. It's one of those trendy places with sofas and huge stuffed chairs, where people read novels and write in journals and try to look like intellectuals. I just counted five people besides me who are writing something.

I stopped in here after buying chocolate for Zini and some good stationery for writing her a letter. Girls are expensive. Very expensive. But hey, that's what money is for.

I've been thinking about what to say to Zini. Leila made it sound so simple the other night, but it doesn't seem that way now.

It's one of those situations where I just have to be honest and take my chances. Trouble is, I'm not sure what to honestly say. It's not like I want to ask her to marry me or anything. I just want to . . .

What do I want?

I want to see her again. I had the feeling when I met her that we had a chance at something. I'd like to find out if we do.

When I think about it, my summer hasn't been that bad. I met a cute girl and got a job in the film business, and only really embarrassed myself twice. Could be way worse.

I saw Athena DePree this morning when she came by the box to pick up Cory. They're going laptop shopping together. Athena is cool. She didn't mention me tossing her cousin in the pool or act like she had a problem with me. I think Athena buys a new computer every year. She goes to prep school in Connecticut and has to keep up with all the newest things. Must be a lot of pressure, being rich. I give Athena credit, though. She has lots of public-school friends and never sticks her nose in the air.

Anyhow, we were all leaving at the same time, so I went down with Cory and Athena and walked up Broadway with them. When we were about to go different directions, Athena asked where I was headed. I said off to buy chocolate, and just as she was walking away I heard Cory tell Athena, "I think maybe Max met some desperate girl in Woodstock."

It ticked me off at first, hearing Cory call Zini desperate, but then I realized Cory was just being witty and sort of laughed under my breath.

I'm running out of pages in my notebook. It's hard to believe I wrote so much. If this was homework, I could coast for the next two years.

Stop. Put school out of your mind.

There's a really beautiful Asian girl sitting across from me in front of the window. She's staring out at the street like she's in a trance, worrying about something. Whatever it is, it's very important to her and not good. The look on her face makes me want to cheer her up, and I would if I could, but I'm just a stranger to her and might stress her out if I went over. Maybe I should just go say, "Hi, I'm Max, the inventor of Coolism. Is there anything I can help you with?"

I'm not going to bother her. Still, it's interesting to wonder how many times someone thought about trying to cheer up a stranger they saw, but didn't make a move, and then never knew if they could have made a big difference.

Watching her worry reminds me that her life means as much to her as my life means to me, or the life of the guy cleaning tables here, or the lives of all six billion people on Earth. Everybody's life is a very individual thing. Actually, I think there are six and a half billion people on Earth.

But of course they're on Earth. Where else would they be?

Dear Zini,
What the hell is wrong with you, dumping me like that?
Don't you know what's good for you?

Dear Zini . . .

fifty-five

It's Sunday night. I have a computer now and just finished surfing for almost an hour. Nothing out there.

Here's the final draft of the letter I'm going to write to Zini.

> *Dear Miss Cabrini,*
>
> *Congratulations. You were randomly picked to win a box of chocolates. Eat them all at once if you want.*
>
> *See you soon, I hope.*
>
> *Sincerely, your friend,*
>
> *Max W. Whooten*

* * *

I already gave them to Zini once, but just in case, I put my e-mail, phone number, and address at the bottom of the page.

Also, since I have a bunch of stationery and have to go to the post office tomorrow morning anyway, I wrote Aunt Ginny a thank-you note for letting me stay with her. I thanked her before I left, but it never hurts to be too polite. Plus, I might want to go back.

fifty-six

Great, great, great. Just got an e-mail from Zini. Said she was addicted to chocolate and thanks for the fix, and would I call her soon because she wants to visit me in the city. She's already talked about it with her mom, who said she'd drive Zini to the train one morning and pick her up later that night, but please don't wait too long to reply because her school starts in a couple of weeks. She signed her e-mail, "Hope to see you soon. Sincerely, Miss Zini."

I figured no use stalling with Zini, so I did it. I picked up the phone and called her. I suddenly got nervous while the phone was ringing and almost hung up, but then Zini answered, and when she heard my voice, she shouted,

"Yippee!" That put an end to my nervousness and I felt just fine. First, Zini said she danced around the room when she read my letter and thanks again for the chocolate. I told her, "It was nothing," and she said, "It was sweet." Then we cut to making plans for her visit. That got complicated because of her yoga classes with Aunt Ginny on Tuesdays and Thursdays and me saying Monday, Tuesday, and Saturday were out because I'd be working on a movie. I'm not sure she believed that until I said Monday was my first day, helping with props. Anyhow, she's coming early on Wednesday, and I'm meeting her at Grand Central.

Great, great, great. I didn't mention Wednesday was two days after my seventeenth birthday. I might tell her when she comes.

When Zini comes. I love the sound of that.

I'm back on my game again. It's the Coolism kicking in.

I called Leila to tell her that her advice worked and Zini was coming, but she was out. That's probably best. I don't want to give Leila the impression I'm so excited I can't contain myself.

Teeny-weeny Zini Cabrini. Love to see that girl in a bikini.

Art is the way to her heart. I'll take her to the Met.
Kiss her there.

fifty-seven

Finished the second day of my job a couple of hours ago. Piece of cake. Everybody said they liked me and would call if they were short on help in the future.

I'm totally exhausted tonight and would be in bed if I didn't want to write down what happened on my way home. I was coming up from the subway at Eighty-sixth and saw Arty Bernstein on the sidewalk. His hair has gotten longer, and he had on a pair of round, black glasses, and he looked pretty damn cool. I called to him and said I dug his hair, and he obviously appreciated the compliment. We talked a few minutes about stuff. Then I said I was beat and had to go home, but maybe we'd get together one day and hang. He liked that idea and said, "Terrific, Max. Call me anytime."

Arty is pretty decent. I bet he'd make a good friend.

Zini tomorrow morning.

Pleasant dreams, Max.

fifty-eight

It's one minute past nine, which makes me thirty-one minutes early for Zini's train. I don't mind. I'm sitting on the floor, where I can watch everybody pour into the station from the tracks and race off in different directions.

Twenty-eight more minutes.

What a week. Earned some money. Got a date with a girl today. I couldn't have planned it better.

Just guessing, I'd say three or four thousand people walk

through Grand Central Station in an average hour. Probably more. Most people are so busy hurrying somewhere they don't even look around. Dad calls people like that worker bees. He says we need them to feed the machinery.

If you close your eyes and listen carefully, there's a sort of gushing sound in here that reminds me of a river.

Zini in nineteen minutes. I bet she brings her sketch pad.

Wonder if I can hold my breath for two minutes?
    Pshew.

I can feel myself getting overexcited inside. That's not a good sign. I hate it when I get nervous around girls just because they're girls. It doesn't jibe with Coolism.

Most of my excitement is concentrated in my chest, and my heart is beating kind of fast. Maybe fuses grow out of people's hearts. If that's the case, I might explode any second.

Hold on just a little longer, Max.